Finding
the
Right Road

ISBN 978-1-952320-36-1 (Paperback)
Finding the Right Road
Copyright © 2020 Ruth Jenkins

Yorkshire Publishing
4613 E. 91st St,
Tulsa, OK 74137
www.YorkshirePublishing.com
918.394.2665

Printed in the USA

Finding
the
Right Road

Ruth Jenkins

TULSA

Preface

When I finished my first book, "That's the Way It Is,", I knew I wanted to continue writing! But, I did not have any plan as to what I would write. Then, the idea came to me to make a series from my first book. So, I am thrilled that this second book is now finished and in print.

My desire remains the same—I pray that my readers may find pleasant, peaceful moments—or perhaps even comfort, encouragement, and an awareness of God's constant presence in our lives. "This is the day the Lord has made. Let us rejoice and be glad in it." (Psalm 118:24)

- Ruthie Jenkins

CHAPTER 1

January–1950

Dear Mom and Family,

You will be happy to know that I am finally settled into my own apartment! I could not bring myself to rent in the city of Eagerton even though that would have been the wisest move due to the college's location. I looked at some nice rentals but could not imagine living without trees and fields about me. I truly believe God guided me to my present abode. After checking out a few ads on the outskirts of Eagerton, I was aimlessly driving about the countryside when I came upon this residence advertising an apartment for rent. So brother Adam, like you, my apartment is over the garage.

I have a combined kitchen and living area, two rather small bedrooms, and a bathroom with combined tub and shower. Provided is a refrigerator and stove plus access to a washing machine. I purchased only the necessary pieces of furniture and other items. I'm about a half-hour drive to the college, so that's more than acceptable. The rent is amazingly reasonable and my landlords are an elderly couple. There aren't any neighbors close so I am in 'seventh heaven' surrounded by all of God's glory of trees, fields, flowers and the view of mountains in the distance.

I've got my college schedule all set and classes start next week. I have a pretty full schedule, as I want to get the pre-requisite courses out of the way as soon as possible. My delay in starting college has caused attaining my degree to be several years later in my life.

Tomorrow I plan to further explore the city of Eagerton.

Love to all,
David

It was late by the time he had gotten his apartment in order but felt he had to write the letter. Now with that accomplished he realized how fatigued he was. He prepared the letter for mailing and set it aside with the intention of putting it in the mailbox for pick-up when he left for Eagerton in the morning.

He looked forward to the following day with the hope of discovering the location of the areas of the city that he was interested in.

*****

David woke up a bit disoriented after his first night in his new apartment. He gazed about his sparsely furnished surroundings that consisted of a single bed, small night table with lamp and one dresser. He smiled undisturbed by the bareness of the room, stretched and headed to take his shower. The bathroom reverberated with his melodious voice. He continued singing in a more subdued tone as he dressed and headed for the kitchen area to prepare breakfast.

He made a pot of coffee, toast and scrambled eggs. When he finished eating he put the dishes in the sink and turned in preparation to leave, but stopped short and looked back at the dishes. He broke into a big smile as he visualized a sink full of dirty dishes and hearing his mother's advice. *It takes a few min-*

9

utes to clean up a few dishes, but let them accumulate and it takes hours. Your choice.'—He chose the 'few minutes'.

He had just gotten into his car after putting the letter in the mailbox when he saw his elderly landlady, Mrs. Weber, come out of her house carrying a laundry basket of clothes to be hung on the wash line. He quickly jumped out of the car calling, "Let me carry that for you!"

She stopped, startled upon hearing his voice. Within minutes he was standing in front of her reaching for the laundry basket and saying earnestly, "Please let me help you."

Mrs. Weber was an independent lady by nature but David's beseeching request caused her to acquiesce and let him carry the laundry to the wash line.

She gestured to a spot and said, "You can set the basket down there. Thank you for your help. It was very thoughtful of you."

"My pleasure. Would you like me to continue holding the basket so you won't have to keep bending as you hang the clothes? I really don't mind."

"Oh, my, no! That's not necessary." She looked up at him with a mischievous smile and said, "I have to keep these old bones moving." She then took an article of clothing and started to hang the wash. "Did you sleep well last night? I hope you found everything to your liking in the apartment."

David placed the basket down on the ground where she had requested and answered, "Yes! I slept well and everything is fine. I couldn't be happier…. I'm on my way to Eagerton to further familiarize myself with the city. Do you need anything? I'd be more than happy to pick it up for you."

"No thank you, not now… but I might take you up on that offer some time in the future."

"O.K., I'll hold you to that." He watched her a few minutes hanging the clothes with her heavy coat and gloves on and recalled the many times he had helped his mom during the winter months as she also hung the clothes outdoors. He smiled and said, "You know they're going to freeze and you will have to hang them on the dryer in the house."

"Yes, I know, but they will be partially dried and"—at this point David joined in and they said in unison –"I like the good, fresh-air smell on them." She looked up at David and they both laughed.

He shook his head and commented, "I'll never understand why you women want to freeze yourselves for a little smell of fresh air on your clothes."

"Of course you don't! Men don't understand important things like that," she replied in a teasing tone.

David burst out in laughter, "No, and I wager we never will." When he got control of himself he continued, "Well, I guess I'll be heading out. You be careful now going back to the house."

"I will, don't you worry."

"O.K. Enjoy your day." He smiled and started walking towards his car.

She called after him with concern in her voice, "You best be careful on these roads. There are slippery spots that are quite dangerous!"

"Yes, I am aware and I promise I will use caution."

The drive to the city was pleasant along the country road. There were, however, several sharp turns that required extreme care. David had made a mental note of them previously on his first time over the road so he was prepared for them. The half hour trip slipped by quickly and he found himself in the city. He managed to find the main business section where the courthouse and Public offices were located as well as a variety of stores and restaurants. He drove out of that area to the residential streets where a small grocery store or restaurant were scattered about. He had passed an elementary school plus the High School.

He still hadn't found the area of the city he was most interested in. He began to notice a gradual change occurring in the neighborhood. Individual homes were replaced by apartment buildings which progressively began to appear in disrepair. There were a few stores also in poor condition, some of them boarded up. He definitely had entered the low-income/poverty section of Eagerton.

Finally, he saw the sign 'Soup Kitchen' in the window of what appeared to have been a small restaurant at one time. He pulled over to the curb and parked. He got out of the car and hoped someone would be in the building even though it wasn't mealtime. He was pleased to find the door unlocked and after entering he glanced around the room. There were long tables and folding chairs spanning the center portion of the floor space. An apparent serving table was to the right and a kitchen area could be seen through a doublewide doorway.

A middle-aged man, with an apron wrapped around his waist, came out through the doorway and as he walked toward David welcomed him with a cheery, "Hello, can I help you?"

David smiled and responded by extending his hand in greeting, "I'm David and I wondered if you were in need of some part-time friendly help. I'm afraid it will be limited since I'm attending college but I definitely would have some available time on Saturdays."

Shaking David's hand the man replied, "I'm Paul, supervisor of this facility and, yes we are always grateful for whatever amount of time or help a person is able to give. Saturdays would be perfect. We not only serve on Saturday but also like to prepare as much of Sunday's meal ahead as possible. We try to be sure our helpers are able to attend their church as well as observe the day of rest. Did you have any preference in how we use your service?"

"No, not at all. I'm willing to wash dishes, serve or prepare food, as well as clean up the eating area. I haven't located a church yet, but when I do and if the time allows I'll try to help Sundays as well."

"If you live near here there's a church a few blocks away. It's The Christian Fellowship Church of Eagerton".

"Really? Which way would I go to find it?"

"Are you parked on this side of the street?"

"Yes."

"Go straight ahead two blocks to Ryan Street and make a left. It's about three blocks further on the corner of Ryan and Smith."

"Thanks.—By the way, what time do you want me to come?"

"Anytime after 9:30. We will be busy from then until we close around 6:00."

"O.K. I'll probably see you some time in the morning. I may not be able to commit myself to a set schedule, as I don't know what obligations my courses might require. Will that be alright?"

"Of course, like I said whatever help you can give, is a blessing for which we are thankful."

David smiled and extended his hand, "Great! I'll be seeing you tomorrow."

They shook hands in agreement and David left with a spring in his step.

He got in his car with a feeling of joy. The next thing on his agenda was to find the church Paul had told him about. The directions were excellent and within minutes he was parked in front of the sign indicating he had found the right building. It had a small paved parking area on one side and right next to that was a large abandoned warehouse. The church had an appealing aura about it. It was a brick building featuring two short flights of stairs, one on each side that led to the main entrance to the sanctuary. The tall steeple guided your eyes to the cross it supported. Sunday School was at 10:00 to 10:45 and Service at 11:00. He felt a strange feeling of an overpowering force drawing him to this church. He made up his mind that this Sunday he would come here for the service.

The day had slipped by quickly. He remembered passing a diner as he was entering the city and he decided he would stop there on his way home for his supper.

It was nearing bedtime as David sat sated and relaxed on his couch mulling over his day's accomplishments. He felt satisfaction in finding the Soup Kitchen and being able to be of service there. He thought of the church and the overwhelming pull it seemed to have on him. Was this part of God's plan? He needed to pray.

> *Heavenly Father, Thank you for your guidance of this day! You have provided me with one means of service and for that I am so grateful! However, I have an intense feeling that You have some purpose for me at the*

*church. If this is 'Your plan' then please help
me to recognize what it is and give me the
guidance necessary to fulfill Your request.
Thank You for Your love and for Jesus. In His
name I pray. Amen"*

He went to bed and fell into a peaceful sleep.

*****

The next morning after completing a few minor
chores he headed out to the Soup Kitchen in happy
anticipation of this opportunity God had provided
for him. Paul was more than ecstatic to see David
since two of their regular helpers were unable to
come. David was good-natured, outgoing and witty.
He pitched right in with a joyful manner fulfilling
whatever Paul asked of him. It was the middle of the
mealtime and only a few spaces were left at the tables
for late stragglers.

Paul was in the kitchen area when he was
approached by one of his regular helpers. Don nodded his head towards David, who was washing dishes,
and quietly asked, "Where did you find 'Happy
Boy'?"

"Actually, he found me."

"Yeah, I can believe that. He's not from around here. He's just one of those……" and Don was interrupted by David asking Paul, "Excuse me, but I wondered if it would be alright if I took a 15 minute break while the pots soak?"

"Of course! Nothing is pressing right now and you've certainly earned it. Besides, you don't have to ask, just keep me posted whenever you leave a job so I can be sure it's covered if needed. After all, you're a volunteer, not a paid employee."

"Thanks." David went into the dining area.

Don said, "Can you beat that? He's got to have a 15 minute break? Just proves what I was about to say that he's just…"

Paul interrupted, "I don't think I want to hear what you were about to say." At that moment they heard some noise coming from the dining area.

"What's that?" Don questioned.

"Sounds like laughter to me." Paul replied and both men went to investigate.

Looking around the room they saw David getting up from a hunched down position at one of the tables where the people were smiling and laughing. As a matter of fact, as they looked about the room most of the people seemed to exhibit the beginning or ending of a smile.

David spotted Paul and Don so he started to return to the kitchen. He didn't, however, just walk past the remaining people. He smiled at them, spoke to them and gave a few a pat on the back. Some reached out to shake his hand which he readily welcomed. He was approaching a man who sat bent over busily eating with his hat pulled down so you could not distinguish any features except a beard. His body language said, 'leave me alone'.

Don seeing David approaching this man said to Paul, "This should be interesting if he makes an attempt to speak with 'Grumpy'."

Paul said in annoyance, "Stop naming people."

David without hesitation bent over and said something very briefly into the man's ear and then continued his journey towards the kitchen. The man for a split second raised his head.

Paul asked in amazement, "Did I see the resemblance of a smile?"

Don just stood in a silence of disbelief.

David walked past Paul and said, "Thanks, I really needed that break," and returned to his job of washing the soaked pots in the sink.

Both men remained where they were standing near another helper behind the food table. They gazed about the room seeing the people talking amongst themselves and an occasional smile. A change had taken place. There were no words for it, just the feeling.

Paul eventually said, "I think I understand now the lesson God has sent us through David. We have been feeding the earthly body, but we needed to feed the soul as well. From now on we will take time to make this place a haven where the people can leave their troubled lives outside our doors and come here to find sustenance along with friendship and laughter giving them a short reprieve from the hardships of their lives."

The helper behind the serving table replied, "I'll be happy to spread the word to the others."

"What do you think he said to the Grump—I mean the guy?" Don asked Paul.

"I don't know. I can't think of anything that could make him almost smile. I just might ask David." Paul went into the kitchen and walked over to David.

"You don't have to answer this question if you don't want to. I will fully understand. I just can't imagine what you said to the last man to cause him to practically smile."

David turned to Paul with a mischievous look in his eyes. "I just told him I had best get back to work since my ogre of a boss was looking at me."

"Ogre of a boss!" Paul shouted and then burst out laughing.

David stayed until everything was cleaned up and ready for the next day. The volunteers approached David as they were leaving, shaking his hand or patting him on the back as they expressed their appreciation for his help—but more importantly for the joyful spirit he generated.

*****

The next day David was up early and headed out to the morning service at the Christian Fellowship Church of Eagerton. He arrived at the church in ample time for the service. The sanctuary had stained glass windows and a center aisle with wooden pews on either side. There were choir pews to the right of the altar along with the organ. A lighted cross adorned the back wall.

David usually would sit towards the front of the church but for reasons unknown, he found he felt more comfortable to sit further to the back. Once seated, he realized this gave him the advantage of viewing the congregation and he was pleased to see it consisted of all ages. Had it been mainly elderly it would indicate the church was moving in a declining growth.

The organist played the prelude as a teenager lit the candles on the altar. This was followed by the choir's opening hymn as they entered from the back of the church down the middle aisle to take their place in the pews next to the organ. When the "Amen" was sung and the choir was seated, the pastor approached the podium and extended a heartfelt welcome to all.

David emptied his mind of all thoughts so he could concentrate on the service thereby being receptive to hearing, learning, and being a part of God's word and worship. When the service ended, several of the parishioners came over to him, introduced themselves and expressed a warm welcome.

The minister was at the back of the church shaking hands as the people left. He extended his hand to David and commented, "Welcome! I hope you enjoyed our service. Are you just visiting or are you new to our neighborhood?"

David replied in his usual up-beat manner as he returned the handshake. "I live in Danville, but I heard about your church and decided to come to your service. I believe you will probably be seeing more of me. I feel very much at home here."

"That's wonderful! It appears distance is not a concern of yours. We would be blessed to have you attending our services. If we can in any way be of help to you, please let us know."

David smiled and nodded his head in acknowledgement and said, "Thank you." He then continued on his way.

He got into his car and decided to stop at the Soup Kitchen to see if he could be of some help.

He knew with his classes starting tomorrow his free time would become limited. He would need to concentrate on his studies and assignments if he was going to succeed in attaining the goal he had set for his life!

CHAPTER 2

February—1950

Dear Mom and family,

Happy Valentine Greetings to all!

This probably will be short as I am quite swamped with reading and written assignments for tomorrow's classes. All is going well.

I have continued to attend the church in Eagerton. I cannot explain it, but I feel so drawn to this church! I have not involved myself as yet because my time seems to be so limited. I feel sure that I will find some way I can participate and be of service to one of their needs in the future.

I must admit, however, that I do have a feeling of guilt by not attending and support-

ing the church of the community in which I live. Perhaps as time goes on I may be motivated to make a change.

We have had a lot of snow and I'm getting my exercise by shoveling. I try to make sure the walks and steps to the owner's house are clear. They are quite old and I do feel a concern for them so I try to beat them to the shoveling. I have told them not to worry about my walkway as I have it under control. I am glad they have honored that request.

Guess that's all the news—so I will say 'Good Night'.

Love,
David

David had one more chapter to read to complete his assignment before heading to bed. Finally he finished the chapter and glanced up at the clock and sighed, 'How did it get so late?' It was only a matter of a short time when he finally laid his tired body down on the comfortable mattress and relaxed. Within minutes he was sound asleep.

*****

David was glad this was the last class of the day as he headed toward the college building exit. He was feeling the results of the lack of sleep from the previous night. He had only gone a few steps down the outside stairs when a person raced past him giving him a hard shove on his back. The thrust of it caused David to lose his balance. He dropped his books as he frantically tried reaching for a means of preventing himself from plummeting down the remainder of the stairs. Suddenly, he felt someone take a strong hold of him averting his fall.

Once David regained his footing and recovered from the fear of the result of such a fall he looked at his rescuer and emphatically said, "Thanks!"

"I'm glad I was close enough to grab you," replied the young man.

"Not as glad as I am!" David said as he picked up his belongings. He stood up and extended his hand, "I'm David and more than happy to meet you!"

"Name's Richard but I go by 'Rick'. I have to admit there was a brief second when I wasn't sure I was going to be able to hang onto you."

"I have no doubt of that! It's a blessing you had the strength or I might have pulled you down with me." David paused and then continued, "It seems strange since there was hardly anyone on the stairs to cause him to come near me, let alone bump into me. There was more than ample room to pass."

Rick hesitated, reluctant to express what he was thinking.

David nodded acknowledging he was aware of the reason for Rick's hesitation to reply and then verbally confirmed it. "I agree with you! It would appear it was intentional!" He then added with a slight smile, "I didn't think I'd been here long enough to have made an enemy."

Rick, noticing how well David was handling the situation, decided to reveal his other observation. "I thought I saw him standing just outside the doors when I came out following you. He appeared to be watching the doorway for someone. Next thing I knew, without cause, he cut in front of me, pushed you and continued on his way. Didn't see where he went or if he met someone as I was too busy trying to get a hold of you."

"Interesting," David replied after contemplating that piece of information. A brief moment passed and then he continued with a chuckle, "Here I am letting my imagination run away with me. Probably the truth of the matter is: He suddenly realized he was late and started running in high gear, losing his balance as he neared me and reached out using me to help him regain his own balance as he continued on his way. What do you think? Sound reasonable?"

"A lot more reasonable than my thoughts."

Both started down the remainder of the stairs. David asked enthusiastically, "Are you in need of a ride? I'd be glad to take you wherever you need to go."

"Thanks, but I have my own car. Should we happen to meet again I hope it will be under better circumstances."

"Talking about meeting again, I truly would like to treat you to lunch or dinner as a token of my appreciation."

"I really can't make any plans right now, but thanks for the offer."

David quickly tore a piece of paper from his notebook and wrote his name and phone number and handed it to Rick. "Please call me when it's convenient and we can work something out. I hate losing an opportunity to gain a new friend."

"O.K. Thanks," Rick replied as he put the information in his wallet.

They shook hands and each went their way.

David glanced at his watch and was glad to see he had ample time for his next stop. He parked in front of the Soup Kitchen and hopped out of the car.

He quickly went and retrieved a large box from the trunk.

One of the volunteers had also just arrived and hurried to get the door for David. "What have you got in the box?"

David answered, "Since it's Valentine's Day, I thought we'd spruce the place up a bit." He proceeded to enter the building, nodded at the volunteer and said, "Thanks for getting the door." He then placed the box on the end of one of the tables and reached in and brought out a folded banner. The volunteer stood by watching him.

"Do you want to give me a hand? I was thinking of putting this on the back wall facing the door so it will be seen upon entering."

David took the banner and headed in that direction with the volunteer following eager to help and anxious to see what was written on the cloth. They finally got it centered perfectly and to David's delight it was eye catching as one entered the room.

"The Lord says, You are precious
in my sight, and honored,
and
I LOVE YOU."
Isaiah 43:4 (NRSV)

Paul hearing activity in the dining area left the kitchen to see what was going on. He thought he heard David's voice and wondered what he was up to since David was always unpredictable.

As soon as he entered the room his eyes were drawn to the message of love now hanging on the back wall.

David promptly said, "Valentine's Day is a day to celebrate <u>Love.</u> Not just romantic love but all the other components of love. There is no love greater nor truer than that of our Lord and it is there for everyone—all we have to do is open our hearts and accept it. Sometimes we need to be reminded." David paused and then directed his next question to Paul. "If you have any objections to the banner, I will take it down. I apologize as I should have spoken with you before hanging it."

"No David, it's fine. Most of these people are lonely and loneliness makes you feel unloved.

It's a good message and hopefully it will touch their hearts."

"There's more in that box than just that banner. What else do you have David?" one of the volunteers asked.

David reached in and held up some medium sized poster hearts. "I thought I'd scatter these around on the side walls to brighten things up." Raising his other hand showing what it contained, he continued, "and I also have Valentine napkins. Thought they'd add a nice touch." He placed these items on the table and then reached in the box and brought out a heart shaped box of candy with the message, "Jesus Loves You" attached to the top. Once again he spoke directly to Paul. "I have enough here for everyone including all our helpers. I thought a little treat would be appreciated – providing all of this meets with your approval."

Paul replied laughing, "You think I would get away with telling you 'No'? I'd be the Ogre of Valentines' Day!—Thank You, David. It was very thoughtful of you." Paul then directed his next comment to include everyone, "Now, let's get busy or we won't be ready for our guests!"

The warmth of God's love embraced the entire area and all who were present at the Soup Kitchen that evening!

*****

David had just put his cheeseburger on his plate, grabbed a bag of potato chips and headed for the couch to relax and enjoy his supper when the phone rang. He sighed. He was late getting home because of the time needed to get everything cleaned up at the Soup Kitchen and he was hungry and tired. He was tempted not to answer but knew he could not do that. Someone was calling him for a reason. He needed to answer. He put his supper on the kitchen table and went and picked up the phone.

"Hello! This is David."

"David, I do hope I haven't disturbed you. I know it's late but when we noticed your lights, Leonard insisted I call."

"No, you did not disturb me. Is anything wrong?" David felt concern since this was his elderly landlady, Mrs. Weber.

"No nothing is wrong. It's just that Leonard and I have wanted to invite you for a home-cooked supper in appreciation for getting the new faucets for the bathroom sink and installing them. Since you refuse to take any compensation, Leonard thought this would be a treat for you and has been badgering me to contact you. You are a hard person to catch up with. Anyway, I don't imagine you have time to fuss much with your meals." That comment caused David's eyes to shift to his cooling cheeseburger and he thought *'no truer words were spoken'*. Mrs. Weber continued, "You can choose the night and time. We both hope you will accept."

"Wow! I can't think of anything I would enjoy more! Yes, I will gladly accept."

"Wonderful! Choose your night and time."

David thought a moment and then answered, "How about Thursday at 6:00? Please do not do any extra fussing—just a simple home-cooked meal will hit the spot!" He quickly added, "If there is such a thing as a 'simple home cooked' meal?—which I seriously doubt."

"In answer to your question—Yes, there is such a thing and Thursday will be fine. We will see you then. Again, I apologize for calling so late but we just never seem to be able to catch up with you. Good night David. Get some rest."

"Good night and thanks."

David retrieved his supper and settled on the couch. He bit into his now cool burger and thought about the treat he would be enjoying come Thursday night.

*****

David parked the car and rushed to his apartment. Just as things would have it, he was running late of all nights – his home cooked meal night! He took a quick shower, changed his clothes, grabbed the box of candy from the table and hurried to his landlord's home. Mr. Weber came to the door upon David's ringing the bell.

"I'm sorry I'm a little late but ran into traffic leaving the city," David quickly apologized.

"No problem. Come in out of the cold!"

David wiped his feet on the rug and entered the warm house and was greeted with the delicious aroma of beef stew!

Mrs. Weber came from the kitchen to welcome David and noticed he hadn't worn a coat. "David! Why aren't you wearing a jacket or heavy sweater?"

David smiled as her tone enveloped him in the warm feeling of what would have been his mother's caring scolding—if he were home. He replied cheerfully, "It's only a short distance from my place to here. I hardly felt the cold."

She shook her head in defeat at his comment and then motioned to him, "Come along, dinner is ready."

David, unnoticed by the Webers, nonchalantly laid the box of candy on an end table as he passed through the living room to the dining area.

He stopped short upon entering the room as his eyes took in the inviting table laid out before him. It wasn't fine china but everyday family dishes that made you feel at home. A tureen was placed in the middle of the table sending out that enticing aroma of the stew. A tossed salad and home-made bread complimented the meal. "Wow!" David exclaimed, "This is great!"

Mr. Weber laughed, "Don't just stand there. Grab a chair and sit down."

Once they were all seated, Mr. Weber took hold of his wife's hand and extended his other to David who reciprocated and then took hold of Mrs. Weber's extended hand as well. Joined together in an unbroken circle of friendship, they bowed their heads in thankful prayer for all of God's blessings.

The salad and home made bread was passed around followed by Mrs. Weber gesturing toward the stew. "Help yourself, David, and don't be shy."

David reached over and took hold of the ladle in the tureen and asked Mrs. Weber, "May I put some stew on your plate for you?"

"Yes. Thank You. Not too much now," she admonished.

He ladled some stew on her plate and asked, "How's that? Would you like a little more?"

"No, that's just fine. Thank you."

"My pleasure," he replied with a smile that reached his eyes as he handed her the plate.

He glanced toward Mr. Weber not quite sure as to what he should do. Some men would be insulted by the offer of another man to serve them, especially in their own home. Mr. Weber, however, quickly picked up his plate and held it close to the tureen and nodded. David responded, and then ladled a good portion on his own plate. He put a spoonful in his mouth and after swallowing said in awe, "Mm,mm, Delicious! Thank you—so much!"

Mrs. Weber beamed with delight, "You are more than welcome!"

They ate in silence for a few minutes when Mr. Weber asked, "Do you have any siblings, David?"

"Yes, I have an older brother, Adam, who is a physician." There was an underlying emotion of admiration in his tone as he said this. He paused a moment and then continued. "My younger brother, Danny, will be graduating this spring with a degree in architecture." David chuckled and added, "Doesn't say much for me since I'm in my first year of college and several years older than Danny."

Mrs. Weber emphatically replied in defense of David's criticism of himself, "It says a lot for you!

Sometimes it takes awhile to know what we want to do with our life. When we come to that knowledge it requires a special courage to forge ahead in pursuit of it."

David smiled and nodded in appreciation to Mrs. Weber's support. He then humbly confessed, "I think the truth of the matter is, I had to grow up – something I just didn't want to do." He paused a moment, "I also have a younger sister, Mary, who is participating in an internship program for working with the deaf. Perhaps you've heard of the institution, it's called, School of Silent Listening."

"I have heard of it and it is highly recommended as one of the best schools available," Mr. Weber replied.

They continued to have companionable conversation throughout the remainder of the meal. The men joined in with clearing the dinner dishes from the table in preparation of enjoying the special dessert Mrs. Weber had made.

Once they were all settled back at the table, Mrs. Weber proceeded to cut the chocolate cream pie. As she placed a generous size portion in front of David she said, "Getting back to the subject of school—Are you enjoying your classes?"

"Yes, most of them. Not enough time seems to be my biggest problem."

"What degree are you studying for?"

David had just swallowed a forkful of the delicious pie and heaved a sigh of utter enjoyment. "This is the best chocolate cream pie I have ever had! Thank You!"

Mrs. Weber chuckled at his enthusiasm and commented, "I had a feeling this might be a treat."

"You were so right!" He said emphatically and proceeded to take another bite.

They all continued to enjoy the dessert, lingering over it as they discussed family recipes along with other topics. The visit became extended and time slipped by.

David sat back in his chair and heaved a big sigh of contentment. He sincerely said, "Thank you so much for the delicious meal and scrumptious dessert! I enjoyed this evening more than I can find the words to tell you. Visiting with you has been like family."

"Well, to be honest David you feel like family to us," Mr. Weber replied.

David jokingly quipped, "Be careful, Mr. Weber. You may not want me as part of your family, since I happen to be the black sheep of my family."

Mr. Weber quickly replied, "Is that so?" He glanced at his wife and teasingly said, "Looks like we're going to have to keep close tabs on this young man."

"Yes, and won't it be fun!" Mrs. Weber readily responded.

David had a big grin on his face as he stood up from the table. "I really hate to leave but it is getting late."

Just as David put his hand on the door knob Mrs. Weber quickly said, "Wait, I will get you one of Leonard's coats to put on. It's really very cold out."

"No, please Mrs. Weber, I truly don't need it. I will be up in my apartment in the matter of a few minutes. The short jog will be good for me. Thanks again for that terrific meal!" He gave them a big smile as he stepped out the door and in short time was in his apartment.

He hardly had time to take his shirt off in preparation for bed when the phone rang. He quickly picked it up fairly sure he knew who was calling and said jovially, "Mrs. Weber. I made it home safe and sound. Didn't slip and fall and didn't get too cold."

"You know that is not what I'm calling about!" she scolded and then continued in a calmer pleading tone, "David, we invited you for supper in appreciation for your help. You were <u>not</u> supposed to bring us candy in return."

"The candy has nothing to do with the dinner nor the wonderful evening you gave me. It is merely a 'friendship gift'. I happened to see it and you both came to mind. So I decided to buy it because I think of you more as a friend than as my landlord. It is my wish that you both enjoy it as much as the pleasure it gave me in giving it to you."

David could hear in her voice how touched she was as she replied, "Thank you, David. I guarantee you we will most definitely enjoy this 'friendship gift!' God bless you! Good night!"

"Good night,—and <u>please</u> never hesitate to call me if you need anything."

CHAPTER 3

February Cont. (1950)

Dear Mom and Family,

Hope this finds you all well and not buried under too much snow! February is certainly letting us know it is the winter season! March is just around the corner and probably won't be much better. It's strange, when I was home doing my 'own thing' I didn't seem to mind or notice the weather. Now it seems to be a drag trying to keep up on all the scheduled appointments. I need someone to have a snowball fight with! I don't want to lose my enthusiasm for the joy of winter. Any takers? I'm here and ready!

I don't remember if I told you, but a week ago I enjoyed a meal of home cooked beef stew! Mr. and Mrs. Weber, my landlord, invited me to supper. Mom, it sure made me home-sick!

I had a nice relaxing evening which I realized I was in need of. They're a great couple! You will have to meet them sometime in the future.

College is going along well. I just wish the home assignments didn't require so much time.

I'm still going to the church I previously mentioned. I'm thinking of possibly getting involved with their after-school program which would be more flexible and conducive to my available time. Right now, I'm not sure if it's a wise move. I want to do it, but I have to be realistic as regards my classes.

Miss you all! Take care! God's Blessings!

Love,
David

David prepared the letter for mailing and set it on top of his books so he wouldn't forget to take it with him when he left for class. He took a few minutes to review one of his homework assignments before leaving. There was a possibility the professor might spring a spontaneous test. He was known to do that and David didn't want to be caught off guard.

*****

It had been a long day of classes and David was feeling drained. He was anxious to get home and relax before tackling his assignments. He had anticipated correctly about the surprise quiz and was glad he had taken the extra time reviewing the material, which resulted in getting him an A. It was quite cold out and he was grateful when he reached his car and slid behind the wheel. He quickly turned the heat on and waited a few minutes for the car and motor to warm up. He left the parking lot via the access road leading to the main highway. He was nearing the intersection when he felt resistance and vibration in the steering wheel which continued to increase in volume and caused the car to veer to the left. He struggled to force the car to the right and halfway off the road onto the shoulder. He succeeded in bringing it to a safe stop.

David got out of the car and discovered his left front tire was completely flat. *Hmm,* he thought, *I must have run over something sharp. I hadn't noticed anything in the road… Well, the spare is not going to put itself on—so I guess I'd better get busy.* He was in the middle of changing the tire when a car pulled up in back of him and stopped.

"Need any help?" a man's voice asked as he walked toward David.

"No, but thanks for...." David looked up and stopped mid-sentence. "Rick?"

"David? I don't believe it! Are we destined to always meet with you in dire circumstances?"

"I certainly hope not," David said as he completed tightening the bolts and replacing the hub cap.

Rick looked at the damaged tire, which was leaning against the car, and commented, "Wow! It sure is flat! Want me to put it in the trunk?"

David stood up, "No thanks. I'll take care of it. No need for you to get dirt on your clothes."

While David was putting the tire and jack into the trunk, Rick was deep in thought looking about and observing the accident scene.

David closed the trunk and as he walked over to Rick he sensed something was bothering him. "What's on your mind, Rick?"

"Oh, nothing....just thinking...You're one lucky Dude."

"What?" David chuckled. "Getting a flat in this kind of weather?"

"No. But getting it at the right time is. If it had happened just a few moments later, you would have been on the highway in the midst of fast moving traffic. You could have been in a serious accident."

That sent a chill through David's body as he seriously evaluated how near he was to entering the intersection and how Rick's observation was right on target. He hadn't examined the tire since it was so cold and dusk was descending upon them. Now David was anxious to find out what caused the flat. He would get his answer when he took it to an automobile mechanic for repair. He looked at Rick and affirmatively said, "Yeah, I am one lucky Dude!… By the way, is there anyone you'd recommend I take the tire to?"

"There's a place on Scriber Road not far from here. When you pull out, take a right and go about five blocks and you will come to Scriber. Turn left and it's a few blocks down on the left.

It's Calvin's Automotive. I haven't had any occasion for his services, but I've heard a lot of good comments about him."

"Great. I'll give him a try. Thanks."

Both men started to get into their cars when David stopped and quickly headed towards Rick, who was already seated behind the wheel. Upon seeing David coming in his direction, Rick quickly got out of the car and hurriedly met David mid-way.

David asked, "Say, any change in your schedule so we can get together for that meal I'd like to treat you to?"

"Sorry, but not yet. I've got your number and I will contact you when things even out. I certainly hope our next meeting will be free of trouble. You take care!"

"Will do!" David replied.

Rick quickly got back into his car, closed the door, started the engine, and gave David a quick wave as he pulled out and left.

David noticed as Rick's car passed him it appeared the back seat was packed with boxes.

He also had sensed that Rick did not want him to get close to the car where he would be able to see inside it. *Strange,* he thought as he got in his car and headed for Scriber Road.

He had no difficulty in finding the automotive shop and pulled into an available parking space. He entered the door labelled, Office, only to find no one behind the counter. There was, however, a large bell with a sign to press it several times and someone would respond. David followed the instructions and within a reasonable time a mechanic entered wiping his hands with a rag. He smiled as he asked, "Car trouble?"

"Yeah, I got an unexpected flat. Wondered if you could check it out and see if it can be repaired or if I need a new tire."

"Sure, no problem. Let's go take a look."

Both men went out and retrieved the flat tire and brought it into the garage where it was warmer and had better light.

"By the way, I'm Calvin," the mechanic said as he started to examine the tire.

"I'm David."

"I assume the tire went flat while you were driving."

"It did."

"Too bad. It did a lot of damage. I'm afraid you need a new tire… Hmm, this is interesting."

David anxiously asked, "What? What did you find?"

"There are three roofing nails in a row. Never saw anything like it before! I've seen several nails in a tire but they were sporadically spaced. It hardly seems possible that three nails would fall from a vehicle and land in that position."

"So what you're telling me is – someone placed those nails in front of my tire while it was parked?"

Calvin looked David straight in the eye and said, "Yes, I'm afraid so. That's the only logical explanation. What parking lot were you in?"

"The college."

"In my opinion that's not a likely place for vandalism, but it is viable"

"You're probably right. Have you heard of any similar tire instances lately?"

"No, I haven't."

"Just wondered if it was a form of vandalism going around but—I guess not… Now, do you have my size tire in stock?"

"Yes, I do. I'll go and get it. Want me to put it on for you?"

"That would be great. Shall we go into the office first and I can straighten out my bill ?"

"Sounds like a good plan to me."

After completing the business transaction Calvin put the new tire onto the car and returned the spare to the trunk.

David extended his hand and said, "Thanks for all your help and information. I appreciate you taking care of this right away."

Calvin shook David's hand and replied, "It's been a pleasure to serve you. I just wish I could have given you better news."

David nodded his head and commented as he got into the car, "Well, some times that's just the way it is. Not much we can do about it….take care and thanks again."

On his way home David had difficulty in putting the tire situation out of his head. He could not stop the random thoughts that went through his mind. *Usually, when someone is playing a prank they like to be around to see the reaction of the person. That is where the fun and satisfaction lies. There was no possible way for that in this situation. I did not have a car following and none passed while I was changing the tire until Rick pulled up.—What was the purpose? – It could be someone who took pleasure in causing a hardship to an unknown stranger.—Perhaps it was someone who was just angry and took his or her frustration out in this manner. But, there wasn't any indications of this happening elsewhere.* He decided to ask around at the college tomorrow to see if there had been any other incidences in the college parking lot.

He arrived home and wasn't in the mood to fuss with supper. He made a pot of coffee and threw together a ham and cheese sandwich. He settled down at the table with his coffee, sandwich and his books and started working on his assignments. The hours slipped by and he was thankful when all was completed. He leaned back in his chair and stretched and noticed it was midnight. His bed was calling to him and within moments he was relaxing and on the verge of falling asleep when the near accident on the college steps popped into his head. This was followed with the tire incident. *I don't wish hard luck on anyone, but it would relieve this uncomfortable feeling I'm experiencing if someone else also had a tire damaged.*

CHAPTER 4

March–1950

Dear Mom and Family,

Well, March came in like a lion, hopefully it will go out like a lamb. I just finished shoveling and will be heading out to classes in a little while. I expect traffic will be moving at a slower pace this morning.

One of the volunteers at the soup kitchen asked if I would like to attend his son's art showing which happens to be tonight at a local gallery. All I know about art is whether I like the picture or not! However, I will probably go because I realize how important it is to the artist to have people come and see their work. I think this is true of all creative people—to have their talents seen, heard or

51

read by unbiased strangers as well as family. I hope there is a small painting I can find that's enough to my liking to purchase. Next time I write I'll let you know how it all turns out.

Hey there, Danny—getting close to the graduation day and receiving that degree in architecture! Hard to believe it's just a little under two months. We won't talk about how far in the distance <u>my</u> graduation day will be!

Well, if I don't get myself out of here and to classes, there won't be any graduation day for me!

So—I'm on my way!

Love,
David

The roads were, as David anticipated, not in the best of condition. It took him a little longer to get to the college than planned. He decided to enter via the access road since traffic appeared to be backed up for the main entrance to the college. When he reached the turn-off from the access road to the parking lot he noticed Rick's car parked in a far corner. *Why would he park that far from the college especially*

with the cold weather and the poor walking conditions?
This concerned him so he drove over to where the
car was parked in order to be sure Rick wasn't in it.
He got out of his car and went over and looked in
through Rick's front window. The car was vacant, but
he could not help but notice a rolled up sleeping bag
on the front passenger seat.

This peaked his curiosity as he remembered how
strangely Rick had acted just before leaving from the
incident of David's flat tire. It had seemed apparent
he did not want David to look inside the car. David
now glanced into the back seat which was packed
with boxes. One box was half open and revealed it
contained clothing. He then noticed a paper bag
between the front seats which had wrappings from
sandwiches and disposable drink containers. *Is Rick
living out of his car? It surely looks that way.—I wish I
knew his schedule.- If I'm lucky maybe I can catch up
with him before he leaves. I've got to find out what's
going on and if I can help.*

David glanced at his watch and realized he
would be late for class if he didn't leave immediately! He quickly jumped into his car and hoped to
find a parking spot near the building. Unfortunately
this was not the case and he was forced to take the
first available one which was several rows back. He

grabbed his books and ran at high speed to the building and up the stairs.

He came to an abrupt stop when he was confronted by the closed door to where his class was being held, and much to his dismay, had already started. He took a deep breath, gently turned the doorknob, opened the door and then self-consciously looked to find a seat close by.

"Well, Mr. Roberts! I'm glad you decided to join us!" the professor's voice boomed.

David stopped in his tracks, looked at the professor and replied with regret, "I'm sorry, sir. I apologize to you-and-" looking at the student body continued, "to my classmates as well." He then found a seat and slid into it and focused on opening his book to the assigned lesson.

The professor stared at David and sternly continued, "I trust that when, and if you complete your degree, you will report to your appointments on time!" He paused slightly and said emphatically, "Please do the same for this class!"

David looked directly at the professor and replied, "Yes sir. That has always been my intention." He hoped the professor would not pursue the issue any further as he felt more than enough time had been wasted from the instruction due to his tardiness. He did not plan nor desire to extend the interruption any longer by offering an excuse.

Thankfully, the professor nodded and proceeded with the lesson. Needless to say David was glad when the class ended and he could escape from the embarrassment.

He kept a sharp watch for Rick but unfortunately he did not meet up with him. He also inquired from classmates if they had heard of any tire vandalism either on campus or other places. No one had been aware of any occurrences.

He had already made up his mind he would leave the parking lot via the access road to check if Rick's car was still there. Driving in that direction and several yards in front of him he spotted a man walking. It wasn't clear if it was Rick, but he tapped his horn several times in hopes of getting the person's attention. He also increased his speed a little in order to catch up. The man turned and to David's delight it was Rick. David pulled up alongside of him and reached across and opened the passenger door. "Get in. I'll give you a lift to your car. Too cold and nasty for walking."

Rick hesitated a minute before getting in but he succumbed to the offer. "So, we meet again only this time all seems well with you. That's a nice change," he quipped.

Yeah. But I don't think we can say the same for you—were David's thoughts as he answered, "So far, so good. How are things with you?"

"Great! Except for the weather."

It was just a matter of minutes when David pulled up next to Rick's car and asked, "Are you having car trouble? Is that the reason you parked here?"

He could see Rick was struggling to come up with a viable answer. David decided it was time to confront the issue.

"Rick, I want to be honest with you. When I saw your car here I couldn't tell if you were in it or not, so I drove over to be sure you were alright. I couldn't help but notice certain things when I looked in the window for you. We all come upon hard times that for the most part we have no control over. I had occasion to live out of my car in the past. Perhaps I have jumped to the wrong conclusion and I apologize if that is the case. All I want from you is to let me be your friend and accept the help I can offer you. I do have a very comfortable couch available and it would please me if you would give consideration to staying the night on the premise that this would be helpful."

Rick sat a few moments with his head bowed. When he looked at David the expression on his face showed the deep gratitude for this sincere offer of friendship and help. If one looked close enough they might notice a slight moisture in his eyes. The hardship of living out of his car, especially during this cold weather, was also apparent. Rick finally gained control and smiled as he asked, "Does this offer include a shower as well? "

David quickly responded, "You want a shower included?......I guess we can arrange that."

"Take my word for it......You really do want to include it"

David laughed and then said, "O.K. Get in your car and follow me."

David pulled into his driveway and parked in his usual spot. He then directed Rick to the best place for his car so it would not intrude on the landlord's parking area. Rick got out of his car and commented, "This is a really nice place. That your apartment over the garage?"

"Yeah, that's it. God really blessed me when He guided me here." David paused a second as his thanks went heavenward once again. Extending his hand he said, "Here's the key. Gather up whatever you will need from your car and make yourself at home. I need to do a bit of shoveling before I come up. It shouldn't take me too long."

Rick did not take the key but replied, "I'm sure you must have more than one shovel. Lead me to it."

They cleared off the walks of both residences, around the mailbox and the snow that had piled up from the snowplow at the end of the driveway. Rick started towards his car to retrieve the items he would need for the night when David stopped him. "I want to speak with my landlord. No need for you to wait in the cold. Here's the key. Go on up and I'll be along shortly." Rick hesitated, but took the key and continued towards his car as David headed to his landlord's house.

Mr. Weber responded to David's knock. "Thanks for all the shoveling. Come on in out of the cold."

David stepped inside and made sure he was standing on the mat to protect the floor from getting wet.

Mr. Weber shut the door and said, "I can tell you have something on your mind. What is it?"

"I wanted to be sure it's alright that I have invited someone to spend the night with me in the apartment."

"Of course it is. You don't need to get our permission. You're paying rent to live in the apartment and that makes it your home."

"True—but I am also bringing a stranger onto your property and your home. In all honesty I really don't know him that well. We first met when he saved me from falling down a flight of stairs at the college. All I know is that at present he is living out of his car so I immediately invited him for the night without giving it a second thought."

"Oh! An act of faith!" Mrs. Weber exclaimed. She had joined them the moment she'd heard David's voice.

David was taken by surprise by this particular reference to his action. He couldn't help but think – *I would have expected her to say 'so you took a chance'. Both comments indicate a spontaneous action without knowing what the end result will be. However the motivation is drastically different. To take a chance is an earthly reaction. It lacks a true concern for the outcome as well as believing it as a risk. But an act of faith is a Jesus reaction filled with love and deep concern for the person involved, combined with the belief that all will end well.*

Understanding what she had inferred in her reference to him gave him a warm feeling as he acknowledged it with a smile.

She returned his smile and continued, "Living out of his car in this kind of weather! How awful! He is welcome to stay as long as <u>you</u> wish. There will be no change in your rent and do not argue with me! One more person in the apartment does not affect us and we would like to help."

"Thank you. I probably will offer him the option of staying. You must agree to let me know immediately if a reason should arise that causes you concern."

Mr. Weber quickly confirmed, "We will, David, don't worry."

"Thanks so much. I don't feel right about the rent, but I'll let it be for now. I best get going.

By the way his name is Rick...er...?" David stopped short realizing now as he verbalized it—"I don't know his last name."

"That's alright," Mrs. Weber answered with a knowing smile. She had just received further confirmation of her initial assessment of David's quick decision.

Mr. Weber added, "Don't trouble yourself about it. My observation of the young man who joined in to help with the shoveling tells me there is no need for concern."

David thanked them and left. He was anxious to help Rick get settled in his apartment.

However, he was surprised to find Rick sitting in his car waiting for him. "What are you doing down here? Why didn't you go up to the apartment?"

"I didn't feel right going up there without you," Rick answered as he got the items he needed from his car. He handed the key back to David and they both headed up to the welcoming warmth of the apartment.

Once settled into the apartment David asked, "Do you like salmon? There's enough of my left over casserole for the both of us as well as some dinner rolls. Does this appeal to you or would you rather have a sandwich and a bowl of canned soup?"

"The casserole sounds great! Did I interpret you correctly that <u>you</u> made the casserole?"

"Yeah that's right," David nonchalantly answered as he was getting it out of the refrigerator."

"You cook!" Rick replied in amazement.

David laughed, "Have you changed your mind and want the sandwich instead?"

"Gosh no! It just surprised me." Pondering over this revelation he commented, "Can't really picture you cooking."

"Well," David said as he continued with the preparations for their meal, "My Mom made sure her sons learned a few basics of cooking. She felt it was important that we would know how to make a meal for ourselves other than just hamburgers or hot dogs." He turned and faced Rick, "What do you want to drink?"

"Coffee sounds good," he answered as he got up and helped set the table and whatever else David asked of him.

They ate in silence for a few minutes when David inquired, "Incidentally, what's your last name?"

"Collins," Rick replied and continued to comment, "This is really good. Thanks.... I'll make supper for you sometime." He laughed and followed this with, "Hamburger or hot dog?"

"Do you think you could handle a cheeseburger?"

"Gosh, I don't know David, that's asking a lot." He innocently followed this with, "How do you melt the cheese to put on the burger?"

David almost choked on his food as he burst out laughing. However, he couldn't resist coming back with an answer. "You put the cheese in a small frying pan with a very low heat.

When it's melted you put the cooked burger into it. Swirl it around a bit and then plop it on the roll."

"Oh, so that's how it's done," Rick nonchalantly answered as he stifled his laughter.

"Yeah, that's how it's done," but as David replied he could not hold back his laughter. He shook his head and still chuckling continued, "You're good Rick! I give up."

Rick laughed and said, "Well, now I know how to make a cheeseburger. Thanks."

David quickly replied, "You're welcome. Don't give it another thought."

"Don't worry, I won't," Rick confirmed with a smile.

David waited a few moments and then said, "You know Rick you're welcome to stay here for as long as you need. There's another small room that I'm just using for storage. I don't have a lot of stuff so once it's organized it won't take up much space. We can put a twin size bed in there as well as a night table and a small chest of drawers. It does have a small closet. It's something I've been wanting to do but just haven't gotten around to it."

Rick's eyes lit up at the offer but then they became despondent. "David, right now I don't even have a job! I won't stay here without paying rent."

"I'm not even using the room! Look, if it makes you feel better you can help out with some of the chores. Snow shoveling, vacuuming, dishes, stuff like that......except cooking."

Rick grinned at the last item. "If I took you up on your offer those things would automatically be included." He thought a moment and then continued, "But I would consider a weekly rental amount set up as a loan until I get back on my feet. I've got an appointment next week for an interview as an evening cleaner. If I'm lucky and get the job, I should be able to pay you part of the rent."

"That's a great suggestion! That's what we will do! However, I think it best if you don't plan on paying anything until you get a couple of pay checks to build up a little bank account. You will need to cover your on-going immediate daily expenses. You also need to consider saving for tuition costs. Is that acceptable?" David really didn't want to charge Rick but he knew it was important for Rick to maintain his feeling of self-worth.

"That's more than acceptable, it's terrific! I want you to know that I didn't get into this situation by being irresponsible. I had a part-time job that enabled me to pay my rent and add to my college savings towards next semester's tuition. Of course that left no extra money for anything that wasn't necessary. I am not complaining as I was quite happy and content. But then my dad had an accident and broke his leg. My folks were faced with hospital and doctor bills along with three young children to provide for and no income. His job did not pay for sick leave. I sent them my savings and kept just enough for my up-coming rent. I didn't plan on a relative of my boss showing up and needing employment, which turned out to be <u>my job.</u>

My landlord was not sympathetic to my situation and gave me three days to vacate. I am having trouble finding another job to coincide with my college schedule. Hopefully the night time cleaner position will come through."

"Wow! Talk about rough times. I'm sorry for you and your folks. Hope your dad's leg heals quickly...... By the way, I never thought you had been irresponsible."

They finished eating and were cleaning up when David glanced up at the clock and then asked Rick, "I've been invited to an Art showing at The Eagerton Gallery. A friend's son is displaying his work. Want to join me?"

"Yeah, I would like to. I've done a little bit of painting myself. By far, I'm not an art critic—but more versed in painting—than in cooking."

They arrived at the gallery to find it well attended. The display consisted of a variety of oil paintings. The artist had mastered the skills of landscape and still life. His technique was realistic in lieu of abstract. David's preference was the landscaping canvasses. Some displayed covered bridges, lighthouses, and a man fishing. The ones David liked the best featured the results of God's own brush in the beauty of the mountains, waterfalls, fields of flowers and sunsets over an ocean. David did, however, like the still life picture which depicted Thanksgiving with a cornucopia of vegetables and fruits. The apple looked so real and appetizing he felt he could reach out and take a bite out of it. There was one canvas where the artist had made an attempt of painting a portrait of a child looking at a bird perched in a tree. The theme was touching but unfortunately it lacked the skill needed. In time David was sure that the artist would master this skill as well.

Rick and David, after having viewed most of the display, were looking at a painting near the refreshment table where there were hors-d'oeuvres and glasses of beverage. David heard a slight gasp and turned to see what caused it. He barely was able to see around the people in front of him but succeeded in getting a view of a young lady's mortified expression as she gazed down at the floor. He tipped his head a little more so he could see what she was looking at. The culprit of her discomfort was a black olive that apparently fell off of her plate and landed near her foot. He sympathized with her since both of her hands were occupied with the small plate and the drink.

He nudged Rick and said, "I'll be right back." He started to go to her aide but had difficulty in getting around the people in front of him. He kept his eye on the olive and saw her hit it with the tip of her shoe and shoot it across the floor and under the refreshment table. It was now safely out of the way. He glanced up at her and their eyes met. He was about to smile and to mouth the words "good shot" and give a thumbs up when he realized by her expression that it would cause her more discomfort. Instead, he just turned his head and looked towards the wall expecting to find the painting he had been evaluating. He was confronted by a blank wall. Now, who felt foolish? He forgot he had moved away from where he had previously been standing.

Rick walked over and asked, "What are you looking at?"

David laughed and said, "A whole in one involving a black olive."

Rick looked at David as if he had lost his mind. "What?"

"Let's move on and I'll tell you all about it."

On the drive home they discussed their plans for the next day. Since they were both free in the morning they would go shopping for the furniture and the necessary items for Rick's room. Tomorrow night Rick would have the privacy of his own room and a bed in lieu of the couch.

It had been a busy day and David welcomed the comfort of his bed. He was thankful he was able to help Rick. He knew things were still difficult for the family but felt within his heart that God would provide for them. He closed his eyes in preparation for sleep but his thoughts took him to the lady and the renegade olive. It brought a smile to his face— not because of her embarrassment, but of the quick solution she came up with and her perfect aim of the olive. He dropped off to sleep with whimsical thoughts of playing 'black olive golf'.

CHAPTER 5

March 1950, Cont.

Dear Mom and Family,

I have a bit of news for you. I have offered the use of my spare room to a college student named Rick Collins. He's a responsible young man who has come upon difficult times. I won't go into all the details, but I'm really glad I can help out. It's great that he has a good sense of humor so we get along well. He will probably be with me for the next few months or possibly longer.

Rick went with me to the art exhibit I mentioned in my last letter. He made it more interesting because he has had experience in oil painting. He pointed out intriguing facts about the diverse techniques of painting and *the different classifications. The artist was really good and I was pleased to find a 10 x12 painting of a beautiful autumn scene with reflections of the sunset on the still waters of a lake. It looks great on my living room wall.*

We are going to be heading out in a few minutes to get the necessary items for his room. We both have the morning free so this worked out perfectly. Decided to treat ourselves to breakfast along the way.

Other than that, nothing else new. Weather is still cold and nasty. Can't wait for spring!

I pray everyone is well and all things going along smoothly.

Love,
David

The morning proved to be very successful. They found the previously planned furniture and accessories as well as a small desk. This would serve to give Rick a quiet space for his studies. They were able to get everything arranged in the room before leaving for class.

It was quite late when David left the college but regardless he decided to stop at the Soup Kitchen.

He knew serving time was over but figured he could probably help with clean-up. He also planned to see his friend and tell him how much he enjoyed his son's paintings.

He entered the Soup Kitchen and found he had made the right assumption. He immediately pitched in and started cleaning the tables. He noticed that Paul seemed to be troubled about something. This concerned David and he wondered if he could be of some help. He decided to ask, "Hey Paul, I can tell somethings got you upset. Want to share it with me?"

"Unfortunately it's nothing we can do anything about! A woman came in late tonight with two children. Not a normal occurrence for here. She was shy and maybe embarrassed. Her husband was not with them and the children wanted to save some of their food for their Dad. I told them not to worry I would give them food to take home. I gathered the husband didn't come with them because he was too proud, but insisted on her coming with the children. This gave me the opportunity to speak with the Mom. It turns out they are being evicted from their apartment. I guess there was an incident that the faucet in the bathroom sink had been left on with the stopper in. The sink over-flowed causing damage to the floor as well as the ceiling in the apartment below. The owner wants them to pay for the damage along with the rent. They barely can afford the rent and obviously sufficient food, let alone adding on a repair bill. They only have a few days left to find another place and it doesn't look too promising."

David was shocked and angry. "How can anyone be so heartless and cruel! Do you know which apartment building they live in?"

"Yeah, I think she said building 568. I always thought that one was kept up better than the others. Kind of surprised me the owner reacted that way."

"You wouldn't happen to know who the owner is and how I could get in touch with him?"

"No, but I think there is a janitor or whatever title he goes by that has an apartment on the ground floor." Paul looked at David directly and continued in a rather stern serious tone, "Don't get too mixed up in this David. Some of these guys are known to get violent if their business is interfered with. The guy is probably within his rights."

"Well, we'll see about that," David mumbled.

*****

The following day as soon as David's classes were over he went straight to the apartment building that Paul told him about. He went in and noticed immediately that the door to the apartment on the right was labelled 'Superintendent'. He knocked on the door and a well-built tall man responded to his knock. He roughly asked, "What do you want?"

David replied pleasantly, "I'm just in need of a little information. I would appreciate the name of the owner of this building and where he is located."

He sized David up and asked, "What's your reason?"

David calmly answered, "I have some business I would like to talk over with him."

The man hesitated as if deciding whether it was advisable to give this information to David.

He must have come to the conclusion that David did not pose a threat because he answered, "Lester Reardon. His office is 66 Main Street and—I didn't give you this information."

David nodded, "Understood. Thank You, have a nice day."

The man closed the door almost before David completed his sentence.

David was now familiar with Eagerton and had no difficulty locating 66 Main Street. It turned out to be a large office building. He went in the lobby and located the directory. Lester Reardon was on the third floor. When he got off the elevator he found himself in a hallway with individually labelled offices. Reardon's office was three doors down on the left.

He went in and a pleasant secretary seated at her desk greeted him, "Good Afternoon."

David smiled, "I'm David Roberts. I don't have an appointment but I wondered if I could see Mr. Reardon. I have a concern I would appreciate the opportunity of discussing with him."

"Just a moment and I will check as to whether he is able to see you at this time." She immediately hit the intercom button and announced that a Mr. Roberts requested to speak with him regarding a concern he had.

David was able to discern Mr. Reardon's response even though it was low and slightly muffled.

"Did he say regarding a concern or business?"

The secretary replied lowering her voice, "A concern."

Mr. Reardon now mumbled, "Hmm. May not be our guy." He then spoke up quite clearly, "O.K. Send him in."

The secretary looked up at David with a flirtatious smile and said, "You may go right in."

"Thank you," David answered as warning signals shot through his brain. *I had used the word, busi-*

ness, when I spoke with the superintendent of the building. Why did Mr. Reardon bring up the word business unless he was forewarned of my visit."

David was reaching for the doorknob to the inner office when the door opened. A middle-aged man greeted him with a pleasant smile and extended hand. "Come right in."

David shook hands and entered the office.

Mr. Reardon shut the door and gestured for David to take a seat in the chair facing his desk.

David noticed he had obviously interrupted Reardon by the looks of his desk top which was covered with paper work. He thought, *agreeing to see me was a nice gesture on Reardon's part.*

"Now what is this concern that you have?" Mr. Reardon asked respectfully as he sat down in a relaxed position behind his desk.

So, he is going with the reason I gave the secretary. David now realized he may have made a serious omission before coming to see the owner. He did not know the name of the tenant nor the apartment number. This could present a problem. He hoped just the incident in itself would be sufficient. After all how many tenants would he be evicting?

David answered in a direct restrained manner, "It regards the tenant, a family of 5, that you are presently evicting. This family hardly has sufficient income to purchase their needed food supply. You are requesting them to pay for repairs from an overflowing bathroom sink. Instead of putting them out on the street, couldn't you set up a small payment over a period of time for this bill?" David couldn't help himself as his voice became more emphatic giving an insight into his underlying anger. "This involves two small children! It's not exactly warm outside!"

"Are you sure you have all the facts…er…Mr. Roberts?"

David started to feel uncomfortable and did not respond immediately… *was there something of importance that he didn't know? He had to admit he did act without seriously thinking everything through and only on the little bit of information that Paul had told him. Regardless, there couldn't be any acceptable excuse for putting children out in the cold!*

"I notice you hesitate. Let me give you all of the facts," Mr. Reardon said as he sat upright in his office chair with a rather stern expression. "This was not the first time. About three weeks ago the same thing happened. I admit it wasn't as serious as this time. I felt sorry for them. I told them they needed to be more responsible and careful. I know it is hard to keep track of busy children. Is it asking too much to request that they make sure all faucets are turned off before leaving the apartment?… I really don't think so. Anyway, I did not charge them for the repairs nor increase their rent to cover them. I also did not pressure them for the two months of back rent they owed…As I said, I felt sorry for them."

Mr. Reardon leaned forward resting his arms on his desk and looked directly at David and spoke in a slightly raised voice. "However, I cannot continually pay for damages done by my tenants being careless and reckless! I am within my rights to require reimbursement! If I let one family continue to do damage, I have to do the same for all tenants. As a matter of fact, that building is costing me money and cutting into the profits of my other investments, therefore I cannot possibly over look tenants who are irresponsible! So, tell me, Mr.Roberts—what am I supposed to do? Go into bankruptcy for these people?"

David hesitated trying to evaluate the whole situation. *Mr. Reardon did not come across as a heartless owner interested only in making money. Then again, he could be a good actor. I have a strong feeling that there's a lot going on here more than what meets the eye. I really need to look into this more thoroughly. But I have to do something for that family quickly as time is of an essence.*

David shook his head and replied, "I believe I owe you an apology. You are right. I don't have all the facts. But I have a feeling you don't either. Since I feel an immediate need to do something, I want to give you a check to cover your recent expense as well as the back rent and one month's pre-paid rent for the family we discussed. This transaction will be between the two of us. I will leave it up to you to notify the family that they are not being evicted nor are they liable for the repair. Also that their rent is paid for the next month along with the back rent."

"It's not as simple as that. Other tenants are aware of the situation and will expect the same should they cause serious damage. It also could lead to them becoming careless."

"Good point. Tell them an anonymous friend has taken care of these payments. This can be shared with other tenants if necessary and should suffice to take care of the problem you mentioned."

"Why are you doing this? I have the feeling you don't even know this family."

"Quite honestly, I don't. Would you be so kind as to give me their name and apartment number?"

"Mr. Roberts, I am not comfortable with this whole transaction and I am tempted to just send you on your way. However, I bought this building with the intention of providing decent affordable living quarters for these unfortunate people. I'm not looking to make a profit, I just want to break even. The last thing I want to do is to evict a family! Therefore," he started to shuffle through the papers on his desk pulling one out, picked up a pad, and copied information from the sheet. He handed it to David, "I am going to assume your motives are that of a good samaritan. Here is your requested information as well as the amount and to whom your check should be made out to."

David reached into his inside jacket pocket and withdrew his checkbook. He took the paper from Mr. Reardon thanking him and proceeded to write the check He stood up and commented as he gave the check to Mr. Reardon, "Believe me my sentiments are the same as yours."

"I sincerely hope so!" Reardon emphatically answered.

David started to turn to leave, but stopped and in a teasing manner said, "Interesting, my concern turned into being a business deal after all." This left Mr. Reardon well aware that David knew of the super's warning call.

Mr. Reardon laughed, "You are very astute, Mr. Roberts. Yes, my building super called me. He wasn't sure what you were up to. He hoped his comment to you which indicated he was worried if I found out he had given you my name and address would cause you to hesitate looking me up. He lets me know if anything suspicious is going on. He thought you might be connected with the Smart Investment Corporation who have been badgering me to sell my building to them. That will only happen as a last resort because fairly reliable sources claim they do not treat their tenants well."

"That's very interesting," David remarked.

"I don't know exactly what your intentions are or what you are up to. Please use caution in any dealings with the Smart Investment Corporation. I don't want any trouble!…and…I believe you don't either." Mr. Reardon's mannerism was extremely serious.

"Thanks for the heads up. I'll keep alert!" David gave a short wave as he left the office.

*****

Tomorrow he would do some investigating. He remembered Paul had also warned him. He wondered—— did he really have to be concerned or was it all just imagined danger?

CHAPTER 6

April—1950

Dear Mom and Family,

I've been really busy. I've been sporadically helping in the after school program at the Christian Church of Eagerton. Working with children is quite a challenge! (Of course Mom,—I know I provided you with plenty of experience in that category) Anyway, combined with the children's help program they have a Friends Helping Friends program. This group covers the ages from 18 through 80+. I discovered a good number of the young to the middle age members have difficulty in filling out work applications. They also have difficulty in presenting themselves in a self-confident manner during interviews. I

*suggested to the minister that we could set up a few help instruction sessions. It would be one-on-one, not group instruction. He was in favor of it and he also felt we should include the Methodist church that is within the same boundary area of this community. I will be meeting with someone from there and we will make plans for both churches and divide the help meetings between the two......
although, in all honesty, I don't believe the Methodist church has a great need.*

All is going along well between Rick and I. Sometimes we hardly see each other since we just do our own thing. We decided it was wise to post our schedules on the refrigerator in case there becomes a need to get in touch. Rick did get the night-time janitor job which also adds to us just waving 'Hi' and 'goodbye'. His hours are 8:00 p.m to 4:30 a.m. It's pretty rough working a full time job, trying to get necessary sleep and keeping up with classes and assignments. (I know that brings back memories for you Adam.) Anyway, I understand he does have an agreement that—as long as he completes his cleaning requirements and there are no complaints from the customers, he can use any spare time for college work. I'm thankful he has this arrangement. He's a hard-working, caring young man and deserves this break.

Miss you all! Sorry I couldn't get home on Spring break. Will definitely make it in May!

I <u>won't</u> miss Danny's graduation!

Love,
David

David had planned on doing a little investigating with regards to the tenement housing after his recent conversation with Mr. Reardon. He reluctantly realized he had to put it off for another day. He had a full day of classes as well as a scheduled meeting with the other church member at 5:30.

*****

Miss Grace Ann Lewis entered The Christian Church of Eagerton feeling a little apprehensive regarding the impending meeting. She found without difficulty the office of the Church's secretary. She introduced herself to the pleasant woman and then was escorted to the abandoned warehouse right next to the church. A portion of it had been renovated into a large room where many different activities appeared to be going on. There were a number of children.

Some were playing together while others others appeared to be receiving individual help with home work.

There were a few other small groups of adults engaged in different activities. Grace noticed there were some rooms going off of the main area. She was guided to a chair placed by one of these rooms.

The secretary informed her that Mr. Roberts would be along shortly. She admitted that sometimes he might run a little late.

Grace acknowledged the information as well as the fact that she was early. She sat down and continued to observe the activities. There obviously was an after-school program for working parents as she saw a hassled looking adult pick up a child.

It wasn't long when the door opened and a cheerful handsome man walked in. He waved at one of the groups and stopped at a table of Sr. Citizens who appeared to be having their evening meal. He was smiling and said in a slightly raised jovial voice, "I see this is your night to enjoy your supper with friends. You're a beautiful and handsome looking group."

"You can flatter us all you want, but you're not getting part of my sandwich," one of the elderly men teased.

"Hey, I'm just telling the truth." The young man laughed as he went on his way heading in her direction. He was fairly close now when a young lady walked passed him. He turned and was walking backward as he called after her, "I like the new hair cut. It looks great!"

She stopped, turned, looked pleased and replied, "Really? I thought it was a little too short."

"Well, not in my opinion. It's perfect!"

"By the way, where were you Tuesday night?"

"Busy getting my assignments done." He was still walking backward at a rather fast pace.

Grace became concerned as he was heading right towards her. She quickly stood. She could step out of the way, but then he might fall over the chair she had been sitting on. She immediately extended her arm and was about to speak when he quickly turned and stopped. Her fingertips were inches from his chest.

He glanced down at them and then quickly said, "Oh, I'm sorry. I didn't mean to cause you alarm…. I was well aware of your presence."

"Well, I had no way of knowing that." Grace replied with a tinge of annoyance in her voice as she let her arm drop to her side, glancing at the ground and feeling a bit foolish.

"That's true. I offer a second apology, it was thoughtless of me." Looking directly at her as he said this, caused her to do the same to him.

They both stood a few seconds staring at each other.

Grace was mortified as she was sure this was the man at the Gallery who had seen the episode of her run-a-way olive.

David had all he could do not to smile as he also recognized her. Not wanting to cause her any further embarrassment he introduced himself. "I'm David and I assume you are…." He did not know her first name and he hesitated, but when she did not reveal it, he continued, "Miss. Lewis?"

"Yes, and you are David……?" She felt the need to know his last name and was not in favor of quickly starting on a first name basis.

"Oh! Sorry…last name's Roberts, but… I don't answer very quickly to that."

"I'll try to keep that in mind. – Well, shall we get down to business?" Grace did not intentionally mean this statement to come out demanding with an inkling of annoyance.

David paused, concerned with the underlying tone of her reply and answered with, "Please do me a favor and stay right where you are."

"What?" she replied confused.

He walked a short distance away from her. He then turned and with a pleasant smile walked toward her extending his hand and politely said, "I'm David Roberts and I believe you are Miss. Lewis. I'm pleased to meet you and look forward to working together on this important project."

She returned his smile realizing this was his way of saying—let's start over again. She found herself more than willing to do so as her annoyance with him had dissipated.

He ushered her into the room they were standing by and left the door open. "There will be less noise and distraction in here," he commented.

It was a medium sized room with an open folding table and four chairs set around it. There were a couple of folding tables and chairs leaning against one of the walls. A small cabinet with several drawers stood in one corner. Other than these items, the room was bare. Grace went over and sat down at the table. She reached into her handbag and brought out a small pad and flipped it open to a written page.

David sat down across from her at the table. A slight smile crossed his face when he saw the pad, but he kept silent. He decided to let her take the lead.

Grace realized he wasn't going to say anything so she started the conversation. "We need to set up a plan with regards to how we will implement this program. I felt making a list was a good way to begin. Do you agree?"

"Definitely," David affirmed. "I see you already have a written list. That's great. We can compare your written list with my mental list." He shrugged his shoulders and looked at her sheepishly, "I didn't write mine down."

"That's alright. I can read mine and you can let me know if you agree, as well as adding your suggestions and ideas. Shall I begin?"

"Please do."

"First of all, we need to get the information out to the public." She glanced up at David.

He nodded his approval.

"I think it should be in both church's bulletins as well as announced at the morning services." Once again she glanced up at David and he nodded agreement. "Next we should make flyers. I think one should be on each church's bulletin board for those who might not have attended services." David nodded agreement.

Grace was beginning to feel a little irritated with his lack of verbal participation. *Had he given any thought to this project before coming to the meeting?* Regardless, she continued, "These flyers must be made available to everyone in this area who might like to attend, those in the tenement housings, the neighboring stores and perhaps the library."

"Also the Soup Kitchen and the Food Pantries," David interjected.

"Yes! I did overlook that. Thank You." Grace replied as she added it to her list." *Well at least he is paying attention even if he doesn't have a mental list.*

David looked pleased with Grace's response and with a mischievous twinkle in his eyes and a complacent attitude he said, "That was on my list."

This caused her to look up at him and when she saw the mischief in his eyes and his demeanor, she knew that he was fully aware of her disbelief of his claim to a mental list. She found him likable and amusing and decided to have some fun and challenge him.

"I think this is a good place to switch and compare your mental list with my written one."

"Really? I thought things were going along quite nicely."

She replied remorsefully having difficulty not to smile. "Well, I felt I was taking over and not giving you full opportunity to express your thoughts and opinions.".... *This should be interesting to see what he comes up with as his next item on his 'mental list'.*

David almost laughed surmising what she was up to and replied in agreement, "O.K." He paused slightly and smiling he continued emphasizing, "Next on my list is planning the flyers. We need to decide on the dates, times, place, and make it clear the service is free and available to anyone who wishes to attend. Then we need to get the flyers printed and decide on the manner of distribution."

"I agree," Grace replied seriously.... *Well maybe I am wrong. It does seem as if he has a list after all.*

David got up and went to the cabinet and took out some 8x12 sheets of paper, some pens, pencils and a few markers. He brought them over to the table and reseated himself. "Let's get started. First, we need to make the list of the information we want on the flyer. Next, plan the layout."

They worked together well and in a reasonable time they had an eye-catching and informative flyer. David offered to take care of getting the number of copies they had decided on, and when he had them, he would notify Grace. They would then set up another meeting and finalize plans.

Grace had to admit she thoroughly enjoyed working with him. She found herself looking forward to their next meeting.

David also was pleased that in spite of their initial misunderstandings they had progressed to a good working team.

It was almost 7:00 pm when they both left the church and headed home. David had left Eagerton and was on the country road leading to his apartment. He was nearing the spot where there was a slight curve prior to a small bridge over a brook which was followed by a rather sharp turn. He noticed a car in his mirror which appeared to be gaining speed as it followed him. It caught up with him just as he entered the bridge. It swerved out and started to pass him, increasing speed and then crowding David causing him to veer to the left to avoid being side-swiped. He was fortunate to get over the bridge thereby avoiding going off and into the brook below. However, he now was on the edge of the road and the sharp turn was upon him. The front tires hit the ditch making turning next to impossible. He went off the road and hitting his brakes he managed to stop the car. He sat immobilized staring out the windshield. All he could see was the trunk of a large oak tree which was inches from his front bumper!

A banging on the driver's side window brought him out of his daze. He wound the window down to see an anxious Rick gazing in at him.

"Are you O.K.? What happened?"

"Someone came along and it was quite apparent he was trying to side-swipe me and it caused me to drive off the road."

Rick shook his head, "Gee David, I think you should report these incidents to the police."

"I don't have anything substantial to report with the exception of this past episode. It all happened so fast I can't even tell you the color of the car, or if the driver was a man or a woman, let alone anything else about it. They would have no way of finding out who it was." David got out of the car and examined the situation. "I need a tow truck to get out of here. How about giving me a ride home?"

"Sure, come on. I'm parked off the road before the bridge."

"Hey, aren't you kind of late? Shouldn't you be on your way to work?"

"Yeah, I got held up at the college. I have to make a quick change and hit the road," he answered as they both got into the car and headed for home.

"I hope I haven't caused you to be late."

"Nope, I can make it."

Rick was off to work within minutes after they got to the apartment.

David had called Calvin's Automotive who sent a tow truck to get his car back on the road. They examined the car and there had been no damage done for which David was thankful.

David finally sat down on the couch to relax a few minutes before tackling his last assignment. It had been quite an interesting day. His classes had lasted until late afternoon taking him directly to his meeting with Miss Lewis. *Hmmm...* He enjoyed her sense of humor and smiled thinking back to when she suggested to switch to his mental list ... *I think she's still not sure whether I was bluffing or not.... She hasn't told me her first name as yet, but I believe she will at our next meeting.*

He sat quietly for awhile longer and then began to think about the accident and tried to figure out some reasonable explanation for the occurrences that had happened since he came to Eagerton. *Let's see, is there a common thread?....* He sat up straight as one name popped into his head—*Rick!?...He showed up at every incident!...*He immediately went into denial. *No, No, can't be! If he wanted to hurt me why did he stop me from falling down the stairs?...*Doubts crept in ...*Maybe that was to make friends with me, then he would know personal details—like the dangerous spot on the road to my apartment and—was it just a coincidence he was running late making him just in time for my accident. I must admit he also had access to my car in the college parking lot and showed up at that near accident as well...... But...he would have needed an accomplice—the man who pushed me on the stairs and the driver of today's car.*

He sat pondering over these thoughts and searching his inner feelings. Finally, he came to a conclusion. *I'm fairly sure it's not Rick even though it appears that way!* He thought a few minutes and came up with: *Mr. Reardon of the tenement house and Paul's warning about not getting involved with that situation.—No, that doesn't work—The stair incident and the flat tire came <u>before</u> the problem at the tenement house...* He sat quietly a few more minutes and came to a final conclusion—*Ironically as it is, they were all* *coincidences! I am just being paranoid. Time to get up and complete my assignments and get to bed!*

Which is what he did—but way in the back of his mind there still remained a nagging doubt—not necessarily about Rick—but that some unknown person wanted to injure him or worse!

CHAPTER 7

April 1950 Continued

Dear Mom and family,

I can't believe that April is almost over and finals will be coming in a matter of a week or two. If all goes well I will have one semester under my belt. Guess I'm finally on the road to reaching my goal.

Remember I mentioned in my last letter about providing some help sessions? Both churches agreed and I met with a young lady whose name is Miss Lewis. I don't know her first name since she wishes to use only our last names. I find this a bit difficult as I am so used to being just David....O.K... Brothers of mine—I know your making wise cracks like—David's lost his touch and etc.—but

I tell you this—by the time this project has ended we will be on a first name basis!

We accomplished a lot and have the ground work planned out. Once I get the flyers made we will have another brief meeting to finalize a few details and be ready for our first session which will be the beginning of June. Due to finals, and I'm not sure of the date of Danny's graduation, we decided it best to start in June. We will run it four Saturdays, two at each Church. Not sure of what kind of response we will get.

Nothing else new here. Hope this finds you <u>all</u> well, happy and enjoying the spring weather!

Love,
David

David prepared the letter to put in the mail box upon leaving. He had a busy day ahead. He planned to drop the flyer off for printing and to do some investigating of the tenement buildings in between his classes. He had an uneasy feeling partially caused by Mr. Reardon's comment inferring that the Smart Investment Corporation might be taking advantage of their tenants and not providing proper care of the apartments. Also, what caused the remarks suggesting that any interference could result in some kind of revenge. He also wanted to speak with the family who was originally meant to be evicted. He sensed there was more to that story than what he had been told.

His first class was over and he immediately went to the printers and dropped off the flyer as a priority. He now proceeded to the tenement houses. He had approximately two and a half hours before his next class.

He decided he would like to delve into the full story from the family who got him initially involved. He went directly to their apartment and knocked hoping someone would be home.

"Coming," a female voice called and within minutes the door was opened. The woman looked blankly at David waiting for him to speak.

"Hi! I'm David and I help at the Soup Kitchen with Paul. He happened to mention to me your visit of a few nights ago."

She looked at him skeptically, "Why are you here? Did he send you?"

"I don't quite know how to explain, except he did reveal to me your situation and I keep having this feeling that there is more to your story. I'm looking into how these apartments are kept and how the tenants are treated."

She stood quietly looking at him and it was apparent she was evaluating what he had said and what his intentions were. She finally spoke, "I find it interesting that you sense there is something I did not reveal and—you are right. The first incident shocked me as we always keep the sink stopper on the top of the medicine cabinet as a precautionary measure even though the children are not allowed to play with water in the sink. I thought perhaps we had slipped up and left the stopper in as well as the water running which in time would overflow. However, the second time I know the stopper was on top of the cabinet and the water wasn't running. After the first incident we <u>always checked the sinks as the last thing before leaving the apartment.</u> Someone got into our apartment and did this. I didn't say anything because I knew no one would believe me."

"I can understand that as I assume nothing in the apartment was disturbed or missing. Am I right?"

"Yes. I know it doesn't make any sense."

"Thank you for telling me this. I want you to know I believe you and I also believe you were not responsible the first time either." He smiled and said, "Have a good day!"

She slowly shut the door bewildered by his last comment, but reveling in the good feeling that apparently someone believed her.

He spoke with several other tenants and they indicated they were satisfied with the care of their apartments as well as the building in general. It appeared that Mr. Reardon was an honest and caring man. David checked his watch and realized there wasn't sufficient time to investigate the apartment buildings owned by the Smart Investment Corporation. He could possibly speak with a few people but was afraid he might get involved and he did not want to be late for class.

He left the college at the end of his last class for the day and went directly back to see what information he could glean regarding the other buildings. His strategy was to speak with people he saw going into and coming out from the several buildings.

The first person seemed reluctant to talk with him. David' s manner was pleasant, laid back and sent the message that he was sincerely concerned regarding the conditions of the living quarters. The person finally gave in and said, "They're O.K. I'm lucky to have some place to live," and he quickly walked away.

Another response was, "No point in complaining, it's all I can afford."

David had an uneasy feeling that he was being watched. He glanced about but did not spot anyone suspicious. He also had sensed that the few people he spoke with seemed wary. It was getting late and he devised another plan. He would head home now and tomorrow he would pick up the flyers which would provide him with a good reason to be speaking with the people.

They would also serve for a reason to enter the buildings.

When he got home he looked up Miss Lewis' number. They had exchanged phone numbers knowing it would be necessary to be able to contact each other with regards to the project they were working on. He dialed her number.

She picked up the phone after a few rings. "Hello."

David spoke up immediately, "Hello, this is Dav...err... Mr. Roberts. Is this Miss Lewis?"

"Yes, and please call me Grace. I didn't expect to hear from you so soon."

"I'm going to pick up the flyers tomorrow. I thought I'd bring your copies over to you at a time and place that's convenient. Since it's only a few days to the beginning of May I didn't think it was too soon to get the word out. What do you think?"

"I agree. Would it be convenient for you to leave them at the office of the Methodist Church? Or…I could come over to your church to get them. That wouldn't be a problem."

"No no, that's not necessary. It's no problem for me to deliver them to your church. If for any reason they aren't ready, I'll call and let you know."

"That's fine, David. Thank You. I assume you're still planning on meeting at the end of May to finalize the few details remaining."

"Yes. If anything comes up that you want to discuss before that, don't hesitate to call. However, I will be away the 14th through the 20th. My kid brother is graduating college."

"I don't believe there will be anything. Enjoy the graduation and time with your family."

"Thanks, Im really looking forward to it."

*****

The next morning the first thing he did was to pick up the flyers and deliver the agreed amount to Grace's church. He then proceeded to the college.

Much to his dismay he found it difficult to concentrate in class even though the instruction was important for the preparation of the upcoming finals. As hard as he tried he could not tap down his anxiety to return to his investigation.

Finally he was on his way and with luck found a parking place a block away from the area of his intent. He grabbed some of the flyers and nonchalantly started to hand them out to people passing by. He smiled as he gave it to them explaining the program and answering any of their questions. When he reached the block of the tenement buildings, he would add on the end of his explanation a simple question, "Are you satisfied with the care and upkeep of where you are living?" Caught up in the previous part of the conversation, several automatically answered, "No, not really." A few cringed, looked about and quickly walked away emphasizing their thanks for his help as they waved the flyers. It was apparent if anyone was watching they wanted them to be convinced that the flyer was the only item discussed.

David looked around to see if anyone appeared to be watching him. Once again he did not see anyone suspicious so he quickly entered one of the Smart Investment Buildings. He hurried up the stairs to the top floor. He decided this would give him a little more time if someone did come looking for him. He immediately knocked on one of the doors with the flyer obviously visible.

A middle-aged man answered the door and quickly said, "I'm not interested."

David just as quickly replied, "I'm not selling anything," and handed him the flyer.

While the man was glancing to see what David had given him, David continued to speak.

"I am more than willing to answer any questions with regard to this." He pointed to the flyer. "However, I would greatly appreciate your help… I am doing a survey of these apartment buildings with regards to the care of your rental and of the building. Do you feel you are being treated fairly and are necessary repairs made promptly?"

The man quickly took on a defensive stand, "I don't participate in surveys…However, I am interested in attending one of these sessions. Do I understand this correctly – there is no charge and it's not necessary to make an appointment?"

"That's right. You just might have to wait if there are some people before you. Do you have any other questions or explanations I can help you with?" David was smiling and thrilled that the man was interested in the program.

"No. Thanks for the information. I'm unemployed and this might help." With that...he shut the door.

David realized this was a good way to distribute the flyers so he decided to knock on all the doors. He went to the next apartment and began to carry out his plan. However, just as the door opened a voice shouted at him from the top of the stairs. "What are you doing!"

The door he had knocked on quickly shut.

David turned and saw a well built man heading his way.

David responded pleasantly, "Who are you and why are you asking?" Of course he was certain this was the super of the building who had a right to inquire.

"I happen to be in charge of these tenements and we don't allow solicitors. So I advise you to leave." This was more of an order than an explanation.

"I 'm delivering these flyers which are offering a free service that could prove helpful to some of your tenants. I must admit I was also curious to see what the inside of the building was like and even more curious to see an apartment. Since I plan to work with these people it helps to know these things." David, pretending to be naïve, continued to be pleasant.

"Well, you do know what happened to the curious cat?" the man in charge nastily retorted.

"Hmm—I believe…curiosity killed it."

"Exactly! So I advise you to leave and don't come back!"

David replied with a slight smirk, "But—satisfaction brought it back. So—Thanks a lot." He answered in a knowing way and headed for the stairway. "Excuse me," he nonchalantly said as he pushed passed the super who was standing in his way.

David took his time going down the stairs observing the condition of the entire stairway. The banisters were unsteady, the steps were filthy and the walls showed some damage as well as occasional graffiti. He wished he could have seen an apartment. He might have managed that if the super hadn't caught him.

When he got outside he crossed the street and then stood back observing and comparing the four buildings. The Smart Investment buildings had several boarded windows as well as uncovered garbage cans with the garbage overflowing onto the street. The front steps were chipped and the buildings generated a feeling of neglect.

Mr. Reardon's building was situated in the middle of the four buildings. There were two boarded windows that he could see. The steps entering the building were in good shape and the garbage cans were lined against the building with covers on. Staring at the four buildings he realized that Mr. Reardon's building was keeping The Smart Investment Corporation from having a monopoly of these tenement houses. The people in need of these rentals would be at their mercy should Mr. Reardon sell.

One more stop was needed to help in his investigation. He went back across the street and entered Reardon's building. He glanced around and noticed the stairwell was clean and then tested the bannister which was sturdy. *Just what I expected.* He then went and knocked on the super's door.

The door opened and he was greeted with, "Well. Look who's here? Some how I thought I would be seeing you again. I know you spoke with Mr. Reardon so what more do you want from me?"

"I wondered if I could step in for a few minutes. I'd rather not talk in the hallway."

The super stood back holding the door open and gestured with his arm, "Come on in."

"Thanks," David replied as he entered.

"You look like you have a lot on your mind. Let's go sit down." He guided David into the small living room which was sparsely furnished. The Super sat in his lounging chair and David in a straight chair next to it.

"Do you know if Mr. Reardon is planning on selling?"

"Not sure. If things keep happening the way they are, he might."

"And…just what's happening?"

"All kinds of crazy things. Something went flukey with the fuse box and we had to call in an electrician. That was no cheap job let me tell you. We also had a water pipe spring a leak in the cellar. Unfortunately I didn't discover it when it first happened so that wasn't too good. Of course we needed a plumber to take care of that problem. Then there was a spree of broken windows. It appeared to be kids coming in the middle of the night throwing rocks. I called the police but by the time they got here the vandals were gone. They patrolled the area a couple of nights but they weren't successful in catching anyone. New windows are pretty expensive. I still have a couple to put in. Just remembered we needed the plumber for a serious blockage in the toilet drain. No way to know who was responsible for that. To top it off, I just discovered some of the bolts in the fire escapes appear to have broken loose. That's pretty serious. Gonna need some help with that job. Other than the spree of the kids' vandalism, Mr. Reardon has just had a run of bad luck and it's been expensive!"

"What about the other buildings. They were built at the same time as this one. Are they having any problems?"

"No, not as far as I know, mostly just some windows broken and some graffiti." He paused deep in thought. "Now that I think of it, we had quite a few more windows broken than they did."

"Interesting." David stood up. "Thanks for the information. By the way, I do have a favor to ask. I have these flyers." David handed one to the super and waited while he read it. "I wondered if I would be allowed to slip one under the tenants' doors. I would prefer to knock and talk with them, but I don't want to be intrusive."

"Yeah, go ahead slip them under the door. I don't see any harm in that. It looks like something very helpful. They might want to take advantage of it."

"Great! Thanks a lot."

David proceeded to distribute the flyers waiting a few minutes by each door before moving on to the next. This paid off because several tenants came to the door giving him an opportunity to speak with them and answer their questions.

On the drive home David mulled over what he had learned. *Was the Smart Investment Corporation behind all the problems in Reardon's building? As regards to the overflowing sink inside the apartment, entrance could have easily been attained by picking the lock. The other building problems could easily have been accomplished since entrance to the building only required a person to use caution not to be seen. This could be done when all were asleep. Once inside the building they would have easy access to the cellar and accomplish their destructive deeds. But was it worth all this trouble just to gain a monopoly of the tenements?... On second thought, maybe the Super was right ...Mr. Reardon is just having a run of bad luck! ...Then again, maybe the super wants me to think that because he's working under cover for the Smart Investment Corporaton......* However... *He did appear straight forward and that he really cared for Mr. Reardon......*Something kept bothering him. It felt like a <u>warning of danger...</u>... but he couldn't put his finger on why or what it was. He finally let go of that nagging feeling and decided on his next challenge... *If the Smart Investment*

*Corporation **is** guilty of these actions then **I need to prove it** so they can be brought to justice!*

He was now faced with the question… How was he going to accomplish this??

CHAPTER 8

May—1950

Dear Mom and Family,

I'm really looking forward to my visit this month! It will be great to have time with everyone and not be bogged down with thoughts of class assignments etc. Of course, Danny's graduation is at the top of the list! Where did the time go? I want you to know Danny you are a great younger brother! Several of my friends were always complaining of what a pest their kid brother was. Never could say that about you! You always respected the fact I was older and sometimes I needed my own space. We have had a lot of great times together! Seems like it was just yesterday when you registered for your fresh-

man year! I'm proud of you Danny, you're a fine young man with a great career ahead... Listen to me rambling on......I sound like an old man reminiscing about the past.

Since Rick has a full time job he won't be going home for the summer. This will give him a good opportunity to boost his bank account without having any large expenditures. I'm hoping I might be able to add on a couple of days to my stay since he'll be here looking after things. Of course it will depend on when the summer semester starts and if something comes up and I'm needed here.

In a little while I will be heading out to take my final in English Comp. I should have all my finals done by the end of the week. Hope the results get posted quickly.

Praying all is well with everyone! Be seeing you soon!

(P.S. To my brothers-Like I said,—I'm on a first name basis with the young woman I am working with. Her name is Grace.)

Love,
David

David sat relaxed on the couch as he looked over his notes. It was a bit early but he finally decided to leave for the college so he could have a leisurely drive. This time of the year he enjoyed the ambiance of the back country road. He smiled to himself as he approached a small residence and noticed an elderly lady walking out to the mailbox. It made him think of his mom. He passed the driveway and glanced in his rearview mirror just in time to see the woman fall. He quickly stopped, put his flashers on and backed up into the driveway and parked. He jumped out of the car and ran to her. She was sitting up by the time he reached her.

He knelt down beside her and his voice revealed his concern but it also was calming and reassuring even though his heart was doing double-time. "Are you alright? Do you have any pain?"

"I think I'm just shook up a bit. My right arm does hurt some," she answered in a shaking voice.

"Do you hurt any place else…like your hip, your side or your head?"

"No, No. Just my arm a bit. Would you please help me up?"

"You're sure nothing else hurts?"

"Yes."

"First tell me—are you alone or is there someone else in the house?"

"I'm alone."

Nervous about causing further injury he insisted, "You must let me know if anything else hurts as I help you up. Agreed?" He knew from experience how independent and strong willed some elderly people could be.

She nodded in agreement.

"O.K. Here we go!" He said enthusiastically as he gently assisted her to a standing position being careful of her right arm. "Do you feel steady enough to walk with my help?"

"Yes," then apologetically she said, "I'm afraid though I <u>do</u> need your help. This is so kind of you."

"Do you want to go to the hospi…'

She abruptly cut him off, "Oh my goodness NO, not the hospital! Just please help me to my house." She kept talking as they walked in that direction. "Once I get inside and sit in my chair, I will be fine. Then you can go on your way. I can't thank you enough for stopping."

David practically carried her up the few steps onto the porch. He could tell she was tiring as he could feel her increased weight as she leaned into him. He opened the front door and she directed him to the living room and to her cushioned rocking chair. He carefully eased her down into the chair. She sighed with relief.

"How is the arm feeling?" he softly inquired.

"It still hurts some but it does feel a little better. It will be fine."

He acknowledged her answer and proceeded to introduce himself. "I'm David. I assume you are Mrs. Dodson."

"Yes, how did you know?… Oh!… but of course—the mailbox… Please call me Gertrude."

David nodded, "Now tell me—is there a family member I can call for you or perhaps a close friend?"

She thought a minute and then glanced at her watch. There was a tone of hope and relief in her voice as she said, "Yes, my grandson would probably be able to come." …But then she quickly with a strong emphasis added on, "There's really no need to bother anyone. I…I'm quite alright." It was, of course, obvious she was still upset and not anxious to be alone but did not want to be a burden.

"Would you be so kind as to give me your grandson's number and your permission to call him?" The compassionate emotion evident in David's voice along with his concerned expression was impossible for anyone to resist.—And so—she conceded, "It's posted on the refrigerator."

David gently squeezed her hand and said appreciatively, "Thanks."

He had no trouble finding the kitchen, the wall phone and the grandson's number. He made the call and then returned to the living room with his right arm bent across his waist and a folded hand towel draped over it. He walked over to her, gave a slight bow and said in the voice of a servant addressing royalty, "My Lady. Your grandson will be here shortly and he was most grateful that we called to let him know."

She sat a little straighter in her chair and smiled at David. It was apparent his little act cheered her as she replied, "Thank you so much."

David gave her a crooked smile and wink as he continued, "It was quite apparent that he dearly loves his grandmother."

She replied with moisture in her eyes, "He's a wonderful grandson!"

David continued the pretense and nodded. "Ah, yes that was apparent as we spoke… May I get you something….Perhaps a cup of tea? If you wish something with it. I do believe you will have to direct me as I'm new here and do not know where things are located."

She laughed and it was obvious she was gradually relaxing from the results of the fall.

"Thank you for your offer. You don't have to wait on me nor do you have to remain. You should be on your way. I have taken up enough of your time. I extend my deepest gratitude for your gallantry in coming to my aide."

Her voice trembled slightly as she added, "I will be alright to be alone."

David continuing his impersonation reached over and took her hand, "Ah… My Lady…you are never alone. The good Lord is always with you."

She looked up at him and smiled, "Of course you are right and therefore you are free to leave."

He stopped his impersonation of the servant and flopped down into the chair next to her. His expression was an exaggerated one of shock and dismay. "You want me to leave just when I was looking forward to getting to know you better! This cannot be !"

He stood, glanced down at her, and spoke using his normal voice and with a twinkle in his eyes. "However, I can tell that you would really like a cup of tea."

She slightly nodded 'yes' and then said, "My, what a time your mother must have had! I don't know if I should feel compassion or envy… Perhaps a little of both."

He shrugged his shoulders and with a half smile said, "Compassion."—and proceeded to go and get the tea. He put the water up to boil and had no difficulty locating the tea bag, cup and spoon. He brought the cup of tea in and placed it on the snack table next to her chair. He left and came back with sugar and milk. He picked up the milk waiting for her direction as to how much to pour and nonchalantly said, "Be careful the tea is still hot even though I put a bit of cool water in to help prevent you from burning your mouth. My mom used to do that for me when I was a kid."

She sat up straight in her chair with an indignant expression said, "I'm not a child."

"Ooops!" David said.

She laughed and replied, "But, I do thank you for your concern… Before you sit down, you may go into the kitchen, first shelf, second door you will find the cookie jar. Please bring me two and you may take as many as you like for yourself."

David looked at her with suspicion in his voice and eyes, "Is this bribery for some reason yet to be revealed?"

"Go or I'll revoke the offer," she laughed.

"I'm on my way," and he was quickly gone and back within a few minutes.

It wasn't long after that when her grandson arrived. He was relieved and pleased to see his grandmother relaxed and enjoying the company of this thoughtful stranger who had come to her aide. He went over immediately and bending down gave her a gentle hug and kiss. He stood up and extended his hand to David and said, "I'm Chad."

David immediately shook hands and introduced himself. He then indicated he was going to leave. Chad walked with him to the door thanking him for all he had done and for staying with his grandmother until he got there.

David softly said, "I don't think she has any serious injury. She said her arm hurt but it was feeling better. I noticed she used both hands when drinking her tea. Maybe she always does that. Of course, with falls it's difficult to tell sometimes."

"That's why I was a little longer getting here. I was on the phone with her doctor. I have an appointment in an hour for her. I want to be sure there's nothing wrong."

"That's great. Do you need any help? I'd be only too glad to assist if needed."

"No. she'll cooperate with me." He then emphasized, "I'm her favorite grandchild."

David laughed and said, "Why? Because your the only one?"

Chad grinned recognizing the proverbial joke. "No, I have competition."

David smiled, "Well, it's obvious why you won. Say, would it be alright for me to drop in and visit her once in awhile."

"That would be great! I know she shouldn't be alone so much but it's so difficult to fit everything in. I try to visit her at least twice a week."

"Sometimes it's next to impossible to fit in all the important things we wish to accomplish in the time available. It appears to me you are doing a terrific job. Before I leave I would like to say goodbye to her since I was negligent in doing that."

"Yes. Of course. It will please her."

When David entered the living room Gertrude looked up surprised to see he hadn't left.

"I didn't want to leave without saying a proper goodbye to you. I also wanted to know if you would like me to visit you once in awhile?"

"Oh! That would be wonderful!"

He smiled as he answered, "Good, I'm glad you agree. I have to leave now so take care of yourself and I will see you in the near future."

He got in is car filled with joy! He thanked God for putting him in that place and at that time to be of help to this lovely grandmother. He then put the car in gear and headed for the college. He knew he had missed his final but felt he should, out of courtesy, report to his professor and apologize.

The professor was not in the classroom so David went to his office and knocked lightly on the door.

"Come in."

When the professor saw it was David, he stood up. "Mr. Roberts?" There were several different emotions expressed in this greeting. Relief, surprise, regret and anger. "Well, what brings you here at this time? Certainly not to take your final!" He had reverted to sarcasm.

"No sir...to express my apology for missing it and to offer my appreciation for your knowledge and expertise which you provided in your instruction of this course."

The professor seemed deflated as he sat down in his chair. He shook his head and sadly looked up at David. "You were a pleasure in class and my best student. I only have had a few times when I regretted my ruling. You, Mr. Roberts, have caused me the most distress."

"Sir," David interrupted, "you made it quite clear the first day of class how our final grade would be achieved. I believe I understand your rationale in your refusal to judge the reasons that would be presented to you for missing the final. I, sir, was well aware of the consequences of failure for the course due to my absence from taking the final which represented half of my grade. I hope you will be teaching the summer course."

"No, I'm afraid I won't be. I take the summers off."

"Well, sir, enjoy your vacation. It is well deserved."

With that, David left the office.

His next stop was the Food Pantry at the church where he left flyers to be distributed. He felt certain there would be some people there who would be interested.

The Soup Kitchen was his final stop. He arrived early which pleased him since he wanted to talk with Paul before the busy time of preparation and serving. He found him in the kitchen getting things organized.

"Hey, Paul…got a second? I'd appreciate your advice and suggestions. After which…you can put me to work!"

Paul stopped what he was doing and turned and faced David. "Glad to help in anyway I can."

David walked over and handed him one of the flyers. "I was thinking of distributing these to the folks but I'm not sure how to go about it. I know the general consensus is that the majority would probably not be interested due to circumstances and age. I thought of giving one to everyone but a part of me feels that those that fall in the above category would think I was indirectly making fun of them. On the other hand, if I just give to some, the remainder might feel I'm judging them and they aren't good enough. So…What do you think?"

Paul leaned against the work table and ran his hand through his hair as he considered the flyer and David's concerns. "I would suggest when it appears most everybody is here, that you get the groups' attention and explain the flyer making it clear everyone is welcome. Then you can either have those interested raise their hands and give them one or place the flyers by the door so whomever wants one can take it."

"I knew you could help me! I'll explain it to the group and then leave them by the door thereby making it completely anonymous. Thanks a lot!…. Now, put me to work!"

It was late when he left the soup kitchen and as he approached his car he could see a paper had been put under his windshield wiper. He reached over and picked it up and flipped it onto the passenger seat as he got into the car. He was anxious to get home so he could relax a bit before going over his notes for tomorrow's finals. He immediately started the car and was on his way. He still had that good feeling within him from the morning's event as he finally turned into his driveway and parked. He reached over and grabbed the paper which no doubt was an advertisement of sorts and went up the stairs to his apartment.

Rick had already left for work.

David got a soda from the refrigerator as well as his notes and sat down at the table prepared to review the course material in preparation for tomorrow. The flyer was lying face down on the table and he felt before disposing of it, he should look at it. After all, someone had put out time and energy to promote their project just as he was doing with his flyers, although he did not place them on vehicles.

He turned the flyer over and stared in a startled daze! A cold chill went through his body! Cut out letters were pasted to the paper which read: YOU'VE BEEN LUCKY. BUT BE CAREFUL......LUCK EVENTUALLY RUNS OUT.

When David recovered from the shock of the underlying implication of the words on the flyer, he contemplated who would have put this on his windshield. *Could it be the result of my snooping around the tenements of The Smart Investment Corporation? The super seemed quite aggressive and indirectly threatened me.* The previous warnings he had received from Paul and Mr. Reardon with regards to these particular tenements came to mind.

He found himself mulling over the use of the words luck and lucky. In a sense they were tormenting him. Searching his memory he recalled the mishaps that had befallen him when he began his college courses. Then it came to him. *What was it Rick had said?....That was it—'You're a lucky dude!' Could this flyer be connected to those mishaps and not the tenements?*

David sat in a pensive mood. Once again pushing away any thoughts that Rick could be involved. *I can't think of anyone who would want to harm me other than the possibility of some connection to the tenements. The flyer must be connected to them.* Once again he convinced himself...*Everything previous to the tenements must have been coincidences.*

Immediately without wanting to—the next question popped into his head...*Was the use of those words, luck and lucky in this new threat also a coincidence to Rick's previous comments?*

This is mind boggling...One thing seems apparent.........Someone is harassing me along with the ultimate plan of causing me serious injury! I just have to figure out who before they succeed!

CHAPTER 9

June—1950

Dear Mom and Family,

I thoroughly enjoyed my time with all of you and wished I could have stayed longer. Classes start on Monday so I have a few days yet to do as I please. This Saturday will be the first interview help session and it will be held at my church. I gathered several different interview forms to give us some guidance in the types of questions that might be asked. Grace was quite pleased with this. So all should go well. I haven't the slightest inkling as regards to the kind of response we will get. I will give you a follow up in my next letter.

Can't think of anything else at this time
so I will end this.

> *Love to all,*
> *David*

It felt good to be free of pressure as he prepared to leave for his trip to Eagerton. He had several stops on his agenda and high hopes of accomplishing his goals.

His first stop was City Hall and he was pleased to have found a parking space close to the main entrance. The secretary at the information desk directed him to the clerk's office. He had a short wait before his turn. The clerk was a middle aged man who pleasantly greeted David.

"Good morning. How can I help you?"

David in his usual up-beat manner replied, "I would like the name of the owner of the Smart Investment Corporation and the list of the board members. Along with that, the dates when these tenement buildings came into his ownership and opened. Also the names of any other facilities the owner might be in possession of as well as their date of ownership."

"This might take me awhile to search the records and compile this information. Perhaps you may want to take a seat while you wait." He quickly disappeared into the room where the record files were kept.

He returned in a reasonable length of time and David walked up to the counter. The clerk informed him, "The owner's name is Hendrik Milano. He bought the three tenements in August, 1947. He does not own any other business properties. I have written down all this information along with the names of the board members." He handed the sheet of paper to David. "Is there anything else I can help you with?"

"You wouldn't happen to know who the owners were before Mr. Milano purchased them? I'm sorry I neglected to include this in my original request."

"It was the Savings Bank of Eagerton. Having just looked at the file the information is uppermost in my mind. I do not know the name of the owner who went bankrupt but it appeared it was several years prior because the buildings were vacant when Mr. Milano purchased them."

"Thank you very much. I appreciate your patience and excellent service." David smiled and added as he was leaving, "You have a wonderful day."

He got in his car and took a few minutes to look over the information. He had hoped that there would have been one of Eagerton's public officials as a member of the board, but this was not the case. He wondered, *how long had Hendrik Milano been a resident of Eagerton or the neighboring area? If he hadn't been and was a stranger-then what brought him here? This was not a large city offering an abundance of business opportunities to lure distant investors.*

How would he have known about the tenements being for sale? I wonder why he has owned them for three years and, as far as I know, has only shown a strong interest in purchasing the other building within the last year? Too bad that there's not a familiar name on the board that I could possibly make an acquaintance with and find out more information about Milano. Well, enough pondering over this for now...... On to my next stop.

He found the soup kitchen door unlocked which jogged his memory back to the first time he had crossed this threshold. *What a blessing that was.* He felt certain he would find Paul here, as he did back then, busy getting things in order.

Paul heard the door as it closed and David's footsteps caused him to come from the kitchen to see who it was. Surprised to see David he exclaimed, "What brings you here at this time of day?"

David hesitated, "I… have a favor to ask."

"Well, ask away."

"I noticed there's a piano in the storage room. I assume it was left there from the previous restaurant owner. I wondered if you might consider moving it into the dining room. There's ample space in the left far corner. I will pay to have it tuned up and I'd be only too happy to supply music for our 'family' here." David's voice was gathering enthusiasm and excitement as he continued. "We could sing hymns and they could also make requests. I'm sure some have songs that are very special to them. I wouldn't play the whole time as I want to continue to help as I usually do. Just slip some music in where ever it fits…I find music to be very healing. It would be especially nice on the holidays and…"

Paul was laughing and had put his hands up for David to stop as it appeared in his eagerness he would go on and on. "If you can play and lead them in song then let's go for it! I thoroughly agree—music is great medicine. I will make arrangements for moving the piano and then you can get your piano tuner."

"Thanks Paul, you're the greatest! Since I'm still on my little vacation I'll be back this evening to help with the meals," and with that he left in happy anticipation of the fulfillment of his plans, sending a prayer of thanks heavenward.

He got in his car and headed to his next stop which happened to be a book store. He hoped they would have the novel he was looking for. He came out from the store with a joyous expression of success and in obvious anticipation for his next destination.

Almost as soon as he pulled into Gertrude's driveway, the front door opened and the elderly woman stepped out onto the porch with a big smile and wave.

David got out of the car and walked briskly toward the house. She had told him to call her Gertrude, but he had found that to be difficult as he felt it seemed disrespectful due to her age. He remembered she had enjoyed his pretense of a servant speaking to royalty on their first meeting and had decided to greet her in this manner whenever visiting. As he approached the house he smiled and called out to her, "My Lady! It is such a pleasure to see you!"

She enjoyed the roll-playing and quickly answered, "Come here, my prince. And let me give you a hug."

He stepped up onto the porch and bent down so she could hug him which he readily returned. He had to admit…it really did feel good!…*Here I am, even though a grown man, I still miss my Mom's hugs. I guess it really doesn't matter how old you are!*

They went into the house carrying on a normal conversation as to what had transpired since his last visit. He had stopped in to see her before leaving to go home for his brother's graduation. He wanted to be sure she was alright after the fall.

Once inside he handed her the book he had bought that afternoon.

She was delighted. "My favorite author and it's his latest book! Thank you so much!" She looked up at him with admiration and gratitude. "I am so fortunate to have such a wonderful prince who cares and is aware of the things which brings me happiness."

"Which in turn brings me great pleasure," he responded with a smile.

She nodded in acknowledgement of his comment as she walked into the kitchen where the Scrabble board was set up ready to play.

"Since you called to let me know you were coming I decided to have the game ready. I hope you are prepared to lose. I don't like beating you, but the object of the game is to win," she said with feigned regret as David held the chair for her to sit at the table.

"Oh, and what makes you so sure you're going to win?" David said challenging as he pulled a chair out from the table and sat down across from her.

"Because you're a gentleman," she whimsically replied.

"I see. You seem to have forgotten that you said, 'the object of the game is to win.' That comment indicates may the best player win. Therefore, gentleman or not does not come into play… Good luck, My Lady."

"Very well, my prince. Let the game begin!"

They played several games with each having successful wins. Gertrude had prepared ice tea and home made cookies. David carried these into the living room where they settled in comfortable chairs to enjoy the treat and pleasant conversation. Gertrude liked to reminiscence about the past. David found it interesting and captivating. She mentioned how much she and her husband enjoyed dancing and listening to music. That gave David an idea. There was a phonograph in the room on top of a record holder. He got up and walked over to it and asked, "May I?"

"Oh, please do! Some music would be lovely."

He put on a record and walked over to her and extended his hand, "My Lady, may I have the pleasure of this dance?"

She was taken by surprise and stammered, "Oh! I haven't danced in ages. I…I…"

He interrupted in a confirming voice, "Well, in that case then—it's long past due…Come on. You can lean on me."

She took hold of his offered hand and with a smile and a look of anticipation in her eyes replied, "Yes, I would love to dance with you."

David was an excellent dancer. His mother prior to marriage had been a dancer and taught him at a young age. Her love of music and dancing became an integral part of his being. He gently guided Gertrude about the room and she quickly fell in step and was transported into some of the happiest moments of her past. David was so gentle it was easy to imagine she was dancing with her husband.

They danced to one more song and David realized it was time for Gertrude to rest. He guided her to her chair and gently eased her into it.

She looked up at him and trying to control her emotions said, "Thank you! I cannot express how much I enjoyed dancing again!"

"It was most definitely my pleasure! I'm afraid though I will have to be leaving after I take care of cleaning up from our delicious snack." He then said changing to a firm voice, "Remain seated! Do not argue with your prince! I will be back in a second to say good-bye."

David quickly had the dishes washed and everything put away. He returned to the living room with a glass of water. He placed it on Gertrude's snack table and slipping back into play acting he asked, "My Lady, Is there anything else you need before I say farewell?"

"No, I am fine. Thank you so much for your gift." She tapped the book he had given her which was on the table next to her chair.

"I hope it is as enjoyable as your expectation is to reading it. I will look forward to our next dance when I return."

"So will I," she said with held back tears of gratitude for those precious moments of memory. "Take care of yourself."

"Will do, and you likewise." He smiled and gave her a wave before closing the door behind him.

*****

The next day was Saturday and the first session of the interview help program. Grace arrived early planning to assist in organizing the set-up. She found, however, that David had taken care of everything and all was ready to go. She glanced around the room and spotted him at a table with a young boy who appeared to be about twelve. The boy was diligently working on a sheet of paper in front of him. Within a few minutes he slid the paper over to David who checked it and broke out into a big smile and patted the boy on the back. The boy responded by jumping up and down in his seat and shouting, "I did it! I did it!" However, his happy moment ended quickly as David wrote something on the paper and slid it back to him. A rebellious look came over the boy's face. David's response was a slight nod of his head and an expression that said emphatically 'get busy'. The boy heaved a big sigh, picked up his pencil and set to work.

"He certainly has a way with young people." A young woman's voice broke into Grace's profound observation of the situation.

Startled, she replied, "It certainly appears that way."

The woman continued to explain. "Harry was having great difficulty with his math and was failing. His mother couldn't afford a tutor so David stepped in and provided the needed help." She sighed and looked over in David's direction with admiration and commented, "It was a blessing the day he came to our church!" She turned toward Grace and continued with an apparent tinge of envy in her voice, "I imagine it must be nice working on a project with him."

Grace considered the question and readily admitted, "Yes, it is."

David and the boy were now standing and both were smiling. It appeared David was giving Harry encouragement as well as emphasizing the need for continued effort and study.

David came briskly toward them with that warm smile of his that seemed to enfold your whole being in a peaceful joy. He extended his hand to Grace. "Good to see you again. I believe we are all ready."

She returned his handshake and replied, "Yes, thanks to you. I appreciate all you have done."

"No problem. There wasn't much to do and I was glad to help."

He turned to the other girl and thanked her for filling in for him. At that moment several adults were headed in their direction.

"Looks like we're in business!" David exclaimed.

They had a fairly good turn-out but had several instances with both of them without anyone. The people who came seemed pleased with the help provided and upon leaving, appeared to be more confident and encouraged.

Grace remarked, "I think all went rather well."

"Yes, hopefully once the word gets around we will have a better showing."

Grace was gathering her possessions getting ready to leave when David commented, "I was thinking it's near dinner time and wondered if you would care to join me. We could evaluate the session and discuss if there are any changes we feel are necessary."

She was surprised by the invitation but, without hesitation, accepted.

They were now in the parking lot walking toward their cars when David requested, "I would greatly appreciate your choosing the restaurant as I'm still not familiar with the area and the various eateries. You can lead the way and I'll follow, if that's O.K. with you?"

Grace agreed and chose a small, homey restaurant with a menu of varied choices. They had placed their order and were waiting for their meal. Grace remarked, "I was quite impressed with your interaction with the young boy. I believe you are going to make an excellent teacher for a difficult age group."

David was surprised by this comment, but was very pleased. "Thank you! You are right it is a difficult age, not only for the teacher but for the student as well. These are difficult years of growing up. Actually…" He was interrupted by the waiter serving them their meals, and he never finished his sentence.

Grace noticed that he seemed a bit subdued as they ate, which was so uncharacteristic for him. She had a feeling it was not connected with the subject they were supposed to be discussing. She decided that she would try to find out just what it was that was causing his dilemma.

"Do you have any suggestions that might make the sessions more helpful? You seem to be pondering over an issue," she inquired.

David responded immediately, "As regards the sessions, I can't think of anything we need to change. The people that came seemed to be satisfied. Don't you think so? Do you have some new ideas?"

"No. I don't have any suggestions. I just thought that might have been what you were meditating about."

"I'm sorry, Grace. Please forgive me. In all honesty, I do have something that I am having difficulty trying to figure out. However, this is not the time or place. I am so sorry for being so rude."

"I'm more than willing to listen,… that is— if it is something you're comfortable sharing with me……Sometimes, just verbalizing can help.

"Thanks. I'll take you up on that offer." He heaved a sigh prior to continuing. "Are you familiar with the four tenement buildings on Bartlett Street?"

"I know what buildings you're talking about, but I don't really know much about them."

He proceeded to tell her about the suspicious problems Mr. Reardon, the owner of the better kept tenement, was having. Also, that the Smart Investment Corporation was pressuring Mr. Reardon to sell his building to them, thereby giving them the monopoly of the tenements. He also told her about the intense feeling he had that a disaster was waiting to happen.

David's last comment caused a look of alarm which reflected throughout Grace's whole being.

"Grace! What's wrong!?" David asked in dismay.

"David, this may not have anything to do with what you have just told me. I have a friend that works in the claims department. He's been with us for a few years. Came from another state. It so happens that his previous company had a policy on a similar tenement building which had a horrible fire. Some lives were lost, plus injuries. It was determined it was arson.

They weren't able to find the guilty person. The owner was cleared and they had to pay the claim. To this day, it still haunts him that he wasn't able to find the culprit. His gut told him it was the owner, but he couldn't prove it. If you want me to, I'll have Pete call you and you can tell him everything you have encountered and found out with regards to these tenements. He will also check to see if they are one of our policy holders."

"Grace, thank you! Please have him call me. He's knowledgable in how to investigate a possible risk. I'm just floundering and don't know what to do next. Of course, I'm probably making a mountain out of a mole hill. But it would be nice to put it to rest."

They finished their meal in amiable conversation.

They both went to their cars which were parked next to each other. Before getting into her car Grace thanked David for the delicious meal and the enjoyable evening. She confirmed that her friend would be calling David more than likely that same evening.

David informed her that he would be following her to be sure she got home safely. He didn't want her to be concerned if she realized she was being followed. He thanked her again and said he was looking forward to the call.

David was only in his apartment a short while when his phone rang. It was Grace's friend, Pete and his anxiety was evident. Pete listened intently as David informed him of all the details and the names of those involved that he was aware of. He told David he would check on Monday to see if the Smart Investment Corporation were insured by his company. He asked David to get in touch with Reardon and suggest that he should try to hold off a little longer before selling. He ended the call assuring David he would keep him informed if he found out anything that appeared suspicious.

David leaned back in his chair and contemplated if he had been over zealous in instigating an intense investigation of the Smart Investment Corporation. He couldn't control the gut feeling he had, but was that a substantial reason for the wheels he had now started in motion!

CHAPTER 10

June 1950 Continued

Dear Mom and Family,

We had our first interview help session and all seemed to go well. I was hoping to see a larger response but I'm grateful for the ones that came. Our next session is at Grace's church.

Since it was rather late, I invited Grace to dinner and was pleased she accepted. We had a delicious meal and a pleasant time.

The minister of my church has asked me to go with him when he makes some house calls this week. It took me by surprise. I guess sometimes he takes a parishioner with him. It probably creates a more relaxing atmosphere with varied conversation. I believe he also *does a short Bible study and one can get a deeper insight with several people expressing how this particular scripture affects them. I seem to have so little free time lately, but I couldn't refuse him.*

Rick has taken a part time job for the summer along with his full time night position. He plans to save enough money for next semester's tuition and send some funds home to help his family. His father is healing well and will be returning to work shortly. That will give Rick some relief from the burden he carries and to the family as well.

Keeping you in my prayers.

Love,
David

As David was about to leave, the phone rang and it was Pete. "Just wanted to give you a quick up-date. I checked our files and none of the names listed on the Smart Investment Corporation application are familiar to me. At this point, I can't make any connection of ownership between them and the tenement apartment that had the fire."

"Thanks for letting me know. I guess I was over-reacting. Perhaps now I can put it to rest."

"Just a minute David. I'm not done with this. I've got other alternatives I plan to pursue. I just want you and Grace to lay low as the saying goes. If this is connected it could be dangerous."

"O.K. Have you informed Grace?"

"Most definitely! If anything seems suspicious, keep it to yourself and inform me. I'll be in touch," and with that he hung up.

The day seemed to drag by as David couldn't control his excitement and anticipation for the dinner meal that night at the soup kitchen. Paul had informed him the piano tuner had come and all was ready. David's fingers itched to touch those keys and bring the joy of music and song to his friends.

The hour had finally come! Faces that had been weary with signs of discouragement and despair brightened as they opened the door and walked in. David was at the piano playing and singing encouraging words of God's caring love for all!

It was another special night at the soup kitchen! Those who were so in need enjoyed the meal prepared for them by caring people. It was agreed that David was excused from his usual duties so he could entertain throughout that evening. He played special songs that were requested. He encouraged those who had almost forgotten what it was like, to sing or dance. There were background sounds of conversations and laughter. Even the volunteers set aside some of the clean-up for later and joined in, intermingling with their guests as one big family celebrating the wonderful joys of God's gift of music! Economic backgrounds and ethnic differences did not matter. It was a group of God's children enjoying His gift of fellowship with one another. Surely, He was smiling down on them that night!

Finally all of the guests had left and the workers prepared to finish cleaning and closing up the soup kitchen.

David volunteered, "All of you go on home to your families or your other plans. I'll finish cleaning and lock up. You've done more than your share already. All I've done is have fun all evening and it would really please me to do my bit. So don't argue with me...Good bye and good night!"

Needless to say, they were most appreciative and accepted his offer. It didn't take David too long to finish the chores. He was about to put the lights out when the piano beckoned him. He went over and sat down, ran his fingers across the keys and then started to play some of his favorite hymns. Sometimes softly singing the words. Finally, he pulled the lid down over the keys and sat in silent thankful meditation. In the silence of the room, God's peace engulfed him.

He got up and took one final check to be sure all was secure, put the lights out and locked the door behind him.

The street was basically deserted except for a small group of men gathered near where his car was parked. As he neared them he sensed there was some dissension between them. He felt a bit uneasy as he drew closer. Just as he was passing them, they started fist fighting and without warning he felt a punch to his back while two others grabbed his arms. They pushed him up against his car. The handle to the door grazed his back. They had their faces well camouflaged and only one spoke in a muffled voice. "Didn't your mother teach you to mind your own business? So take this as a warning to back off!" and with that punched him in the ribs causing him to double over when they released him. As they were quickly running away a different voice called back, "If we have to come again be advised. No amount of satisfaction will bring YOU back!"

David managed to get the front door of the car open and slid in behind the steering wheel.

He sat awhile until he regained his breath and the pain eased. There was no one on the street.

No witnesses to the attack. He headed home as soon as he felt secure enough to drive.

He parked the car as close as possible to the stairs leading to his apartment. He held tight to the banister as he climbed them to be sure he wouldn't lose his balance and fall. He unlocked the door, hit the switch for the light, and went directly to the phone. He felt the need to call Pete and warn him.

Pete answered the phone with a leisurely, "Hi, this is Pete."

David quickly told him what had happened and also related his concern for Grace as well.

There was no doubt that Pete was concerned about this occurrence and reassured David he had previously warned Grace not to do any investigating on her own.

Pete continued to give David instructions, "David this is what I want you to do. Go to the emergency room **now** to be checked out and tell them what happened. Be sure they record it as well as calling the police to come and get your statement. This is…"

David interrupted, "But Pete there were no witnesses! Even though I'm sure I recognized the second voice, I imagine he has a sound alibi to certify he was some place else. I really don't need medical…"

This time Pete interrupted, "David, it is very important that this is verified in writing by the authorities. Also, you stay away from the vicinity of those tenements and as I told Grace-<u>Do not do any further investigating on your own.</u> There is the possibility people will notice you are in pain. Tell them you pulled a muscle or something like that. Keep me informed if anything else develops and of course do not discuss this with anyone else."

"You and Grace are the only people I have mentioned this to."

"Good!. I hope you're O.K. I'll keep you informed. I'm sorry about the pain you are suffering, but I must admit, I'm sort of glad it happened." With that he hung up.

David sighed, gritted his teeth and headed for the hospital.

He followed Pete's instructions and made sure the hospital and the police had all facts of the incident recorded if needed for further verification.

*****

It was the following Saturday and the second session of the interview help program, this time being held at Grace's church. David came early to help with setting up. He entered the church and there was a poster on an easel. It had an arrow pointing in the direction of the stairs informing people that the session was in the meeting hall below. As he approached the hall he heard what he assumed to be the choir rehearsing. He decided to wait until they completed the hymn, but suddenly found himself completely captivated by the beautiful voice of the woman soloist. They completed the hymn and by the sounds it became apparent the rehearsal was over.

He entered the room and Grace spotted him immediately and came over to him. Her concern was obvious as she asked him, "Are you sure you're alright to do these interviews?"

"Yes. I'm fine."

She gave him a look of skepticism as she led him to the room where the interviews were to take place. Everything was set up and ready to go.

David noticed a small table was near the entrance to the room. Flyers were available giving pertinent information about the two churches sponsoring the program. It gave the Pastors' names and phone numbers of the office along with the times of the services. Also there were vouchers for clothing from their Thrift Shops.

"This is terrific Grace! What a great idea."

Grace approached him with regret in her eyes and humbly replied, "David I wanted to run this by you before doing it, but it was right at the time of your injury and I didn't want to disturb you. I went ahead on the premise that if you did not agree, we could remove them."

"I'm glad you went ahead with it." Emphatically he continued, "The vouchers are fantastic! This takes care of one of the most difficult parts of some of the interviews. Appearance is an essential component in creating an exemplary first impression. As we both know a lot of our participants do not have many choices as regards their clothing."

"I agree and I also found that difficult." She paused and then continued, "I must confess what else I have done without consulting you. I made contact with both shops to have someone available to help anyone who has a voucher."

"You are amazing! How thoughtful of you and what a great help that will be for them! We will direct them to stop at the table as they leave."

He hardly finished the sentence when the people started to arrive.

They were kept busy for most of the time. Evidently the word had gotten around about the help they had received and encouraged others to attend.

The session had ended and the room had been put in order when Grace brought a package and placed it on the table in front of David.

"What is this?" he asked with curiosity.

"It's some left over lasagna I made and thought you might enjoy it. I don't imagine you feel much like fussing to make something to eat." She paused, "Unless of course you have someone preparing a meal for you." She realized she didn't know if David was living alone.

David laughed at her last remark. "I do have someone sharing the apartment, but believe me, I don't want him cooking for me!" He proceeded to look into the bag and slid the casserole out a bit. "Wow! That looks delicious and it is quite a lot!" He put on a pondering expression and then said, "I noticed the church has a kitchen and I wondered…" His eyes took on a mischievous glint as he continued, "Since I have been blessed by the gift of this food from a very thoughtful and caring person, perhaps you would consider joining me."

She smiled at his comment well aware of the sincerity underlying his jesting, but hesitated to accept. "David, you must be anxious to get home and relax in a comfortable chair. These folding chairs do nothing to help someone who is suffering from an injury." She looked at him with sympathy and added, "I noticed you cringed now and again."

He answered still with the mischievous glint, "You really think it would be best for me to go home and have to carry that heavy casserole up my stairs. Next, I would have to bend over to put it in the oven and then take it out—bending again……… Personally, I would much prefer to sit on a folding chair enjoying your company as I savor this special meal!" The last sentence was said in earnest, the mischievous glint was gone.

Grace could not refuse him. She did, however, make certain that she put the casserole and the foil wrapped Italian bread in and out of the oven. She knew reaching and bending caused him pain. Together they prepared the table for their meal which didn't take very long to heat. Each said a silent prayer of thanks prior to eating.

Right after his first bite, David commented how special and delicious the home made lasagna was and thanked Grace again.

He wanted to know a little more about her and asked, "I know you work for an insurance company—have you been there long?"

"Since my senior year of high school. I started out in the mail room. Then moved up through the different departments. I'm now in the rating department and taking classes for certification as an insurance underwriter."

"Impressive. You're climbing that ladder to success rather quickly. I assume you enjoy your job. That's really important."

"I'm blessed to have it...... It will probably be several years before there is an opening for the underwriting position. Someone needs to either quit or retire. A final exam is required and only the top two will be considered for the position when it is available. I'm due to take my exam in three weeks."

"No doubt in my mind...You will be first on that list!"

She laughed, "Thank you for your vote of confidence."

There were a few moments of silence when David commented, "I'm glad I got here in time to hear part of the choir's rehearsal. Who was the soloist? I was caught up in the spell of her beautiful voice!"

"Oh!" Grace said blushing...

He took in her whole reaction and realized, "That was you! Wasn't it!"

"Yes. Thank you for the compliment." she replied humbly. She paused and then continued wistfully, "I feel so blessed that God bestowed upon me this gift and knowledge of music."

"Do I hear an underlying desire in that statement?"

"You probably do. I wanted to be a vocal music teacher. I desire to teach children more than just the basics of music. I want every child to feel the joy of singing whether they can carry a tune or not! It's mentioned in the bible more than once to sing God's praises. Every voice when it reaches God is beautiful to Him. Maybe along the way I would get the opportunity to help some students who wanted and had the potential to perfect their voices. Then they would get the same awesome feeling I have seeing the faces of those enthralled by this blessing!"

"You're right!" David said emphatically and the look in his eyes told her he had come up with a plan. She had the uneasy feeling that it included her.

"I know some people who would be thrilled to hear you sing and it would be like medicine to their souls. Are you interested?"

"I think you're exaggerating, but of course I'm interested."

"It's the soup kitchen. I help out there sometimes and if you wanted to… you could come with me. They have a piano and I could accompany you. Still interested?"

"Even more so."

"Great! How about next Sunday for their evening meal at 6:00? No need for you to drive. I'll pick you up. That work for you?"

"Perfect! I'll look forward to it."

David followed Grace to her building as well as escorting her to her second floor apartment. He waited in the hall until he was sure all was safe for her inside.

He was glad to get home and relax in his favorite comfortable chair. It wasn't long when the phone rang just as he was dozing off. He sighed and got up and answered it.

"Hi, David, this is Pete. Just wanted to give you an update. I'm working on getting the authorities to inspect the Smart Investment Corporation's tenements. I have a bit of a plan and wondered if you would be willing to assist. It could be a little dangerous. It would call for a little acting on your part... I really can't see that being a problem for you."

David answered with a chuckle in his voice, "I'm not sure how to interpret that last remark."

In a more serious tone he continued, "Of course I'll help. What do you need me to do?"

"Can't go into details right now. Need to get approval. If all goes well, it should be in the next few weeks. I'll be in touch."

"Hey, wait a minute! You can't leave me hanging like this! At least give me an inkling of the plan."

"Can't do! I'll be in touch soon. Take care. Have a good night." With that he hung up.

David stood there looking at the phone. *He's got to be kidding. Sure, I'll have a wonderful night wondering what I might be asked to do and thereby put myself in danger. Thanks a lot, Pete!*

CHAPTER 11

July—1950

Dear Mom and Family,

Here we are already in July. The summer semester is moving along quickly. The minister and I didn't get to do visitations in June. Some unexpected things came up and we couldn't coordinate our times. Planning to do it within the next couple weeks. The remainder of our Interview Help sessions were quite successful. The new items that Grace had implemented were very useful and proved to be very much appreciated.

Oh, I forgot to tell you. Grace has a beautiful singing voice and she was more than happy to join me at the soup kitchen these past couple of Sunday evenings. Everyone enjoys listening to her! Even the man who has kept his head bowed and never looked up responded with a slight raising of his eyes. It really feels like having a Sunday Service since we offer our prayers and have a scripture reading as well. Of course Grace pitches in wherever else she can be of help throughout the evening. We also had a great 4th of July celebration. Had some noise makers, balloons to pop, sang patriotic songs. Grace and I sometimes sing a duet. Most importantly we offered our prayers of thanks for the freedoms we have in this country and prayed for God's guidance for the President and all those in office.

Well, it's getting late and I still have a paper to write for tomorrow's class. I don't think it's going to be too complicated...... At least I hope not!

Try to keep cool and enjoy the summer days!

Love,
David

Rick pulled into the driveway after finishing his night's work and noticed the kitchen light was on.

He unlocked the door and walked into the living room and found David slumped over the kitchen table sound asleep with pen in hand. Giving David a slight tap on the shoulder and speaking to him caused David to wake up in a daze.

"Looks like you didn't go to bed last night," Rick commented.

Yawning, he replied,"I didn't feel that tired when I started working on the paper."

Rick, glancing down at the table, and picked up the text book that was there. What are you doing with this? Didn't you take your English Comp. final last semester?"

David hesitated, "No, I didn't."

"What do you mean you didn't? I remember distinctly you left in plenty of time so you wouldn't be late and get an automatic failure. What happened?"

David sighed, "An elderly lady fell and I stayed with her until her grandson got there...You would have done the same thing."

"Was she hurt real bad?" He stared at David for a moment and then answered the question himself. "No, she wasn't! I agree with you that I would have stopped and helped her. But, if she was OK, I wouldn't have stayed and jeopardized the completion of this class as well as my average and the potential of qualifying for a better paying position upon graduation."

David shook his head and said emphatically, "You would have gone the extra mile! Don't try to tell me anything different…Go to bed and get some sleep after working the night… I have to get this paper done."

Exasperated Rick headed to his room as he retaliated, "At this rate you'll get your degree just in time for retirement!"

*****

David and the Pastor finally were able to schedule a day for the visitations. After several visits they were heading to the last person on the list. The pastor had informed David that the man was in his early sixties and was wheelchair bound due to an automobile accident. He was extremely depressed and had lost all interest in living. He would constantly ask, 'Why doesn't God come and take me?'

"David, this man is the main reason I wanted you to come with me today. You have the wonderful gift of cheering people up."

"You really think I can cheer this man up?" David asked in disbelief.

"Yes, I do. His name is Harry."

They pulled up in front of a small apartment house and went in and knocked on the first floor apartment door.

A gruff voice answered to come in after several moments of knocking.

The door opened into the kitchen where Harry was waiting for them. "I see you brought someone with you," he said in a rather annoyed voice.

David quickly extended his hand and smiling said, "I'm David and it's a pleasure to meet you."

It was quite apparent Harry wanted to respond in a negative manner. He gazed up at the face of this young pleasant man, and for a reason he didn't understand, he felt a slight twinge of guilt and held his tongue. "We might as well go into the living room where there are more comfortable chairs to sit in."

He led the way. The apartment layout was known as a railroad flat. You walked from the kitchen, passed the door to the bathroom, and then walked through the first bed room and then through the second bedroom and finally into the living room. As they left the kitchen David noticed there was an easel and painting supplies on one end of the table. When they stepped into the living room there were exquisite paintings hanging as well as some stacked, leaning against the wall.

"These are breathtaking," David exclaimed as he walked closer to study them.

"They're just useless items!" Harry replied curmudgeonly.

David walked over and sat down facing Harry and said deliberately, "No, they are not! They are beautiful and reflect a gift from God... I assume you painted them."

"I did." He sighed, "I suppose they had the purpose of entertaining me. I admit, I enjoyed painting them. But now they're just dust collectors."

David shook his head. "They have a greater purpose than that!...Tell me...do you have a problem in parting with your paintings?"

"Of course not! You want them? Take them!" He said gruffly......but then a whole different expression came over his face......one of concern. "What are you going to do with them?"

David smiled in satisfaction as he thought, *he does care about his paintings.* He answered, "I'm not going to do anything with them......but you are!... That is if you want to."

"And just what am I going to do—- stuck here in a wheelchair!?"

"Reserve the use of the Eagerton Gallery to display and sell them. Share this gift that God has given you! You're talented enough to take orders for special paintings as well." David put his hand up indicating for Harry not to speak. "Believe me, your fellow Christians will be thrilled to give you all the help you need. You want to know why God hasn't taken you? It's because you're not done yet in fulfilling His plans for you. So, what is your decision?"

"My decision is—You're a dreamer if what you just said is what you believe."

David smiled and said, "I believe in possibility. In my opinion this is the order of the way one's thoughts can go. First there is the dreamer, which has two facets to it. The fantasy dreamer who dreams for those things which we have no control over—example- longing for the one true love to come along. The second part of the dreamer is for those things like— attaining a degree in a specific profession, a beautiful home, new car, success in finances and so on. Now, if this person pursues these dreams he has reached the level of possibility. He now has some control over attaining his dream, but he needs to put out the effort and keep the faith."

"So, this young man is a philosopher," Harry commented with a touch of sarcasm.

David chuckled and responded, "No, just sharing my thoughts with you."

The pastor remarked, "He does surprise me at times. I'm never quite sure just what he might come up with." He paused and then continued, "I would suggest that we now open our Bibles and take turns in reading some scriptures I have chosen for our time together." He handed a small slip of paper to each of them listing the verses. "David, would you please read the first one?"

David smiled, "With pleasure... First Corinthians, Chapter 7 Verse:7—'Each man has his own gift from God—One has this gift, another that'."

"Harry, the next one please," the pastor requested.

Harry nodded and read, "First Timothy Chapter 4 Verse:14—'Do not neglect your gift."—Harry hesitated and briefly glanced up at the pastor and then finished the passage,—'which was given to you'."

The pastor read the final scripture, "First Peter Chapter 4 Verse10—'Each one should use whatever gift he has received to serve others, faithfully administering God's grace in it's various forms'." He paused briefly and then continued, "So, I think we all need to give serious thought to the message of these scriptures until we meet again and can delve into their full meaning in our lives...David would you lead us in the hymn, 'Blessed Assurance' as a conclusion to our time together?"

David was taken by surprise at the request but responded in joyful enthusiasm ending the visit.

David asked Harry prior to leaving if it would be alright if he were to stop in to spend more time with him in the future. Of course Harry did not reply with great enthusiasm, but if one were attentive they would detect a glimmer of pleasure.

On the ride back to the church the pastor commented, "David, I don't know what degree you are aiming for but, in my observations, you would make an excellent minister! I would be more than willing to give you all the assistance I can in getting you admitted to seminary. I sincerely think you should give it some serious consideration."

David sat in shocked silence, trying to absorb these unexpected as well as unbelievable words from the pastor.

*****

Grace and David were leaving the Soup Kitchen after clean-up had been completed following the Sunday meal. They had fallen into a routine of David picking Grace up and bringing her to the Soup Kitchen since she now took part in entertaining as well as helping where needed. This was followed with stopping at the diner for a bite to eat before taking her back home. On the ride to the diner, Grace sensed David was excited about something and was having difficulty controlling his anxiousness. Grace looked upon this as a warning sign. *What has he dreamt up that will undoubtably involve me?*

Once they were seated and placed their order David said, "Grace! I've got the greatest idea!"

Here it comes, she thought and glanced up at him. *Yes, there it was in his eyes, the excitement of a child who has just received a brand new toy!* She couldn't control her slight chuckle as she asked, "What is it, David? It better not include me."

"But—but you're an integral part of it," he replied in utter dismay.

She shook her head and with a slight smile said, "Go ahead and tell me what it is."

Just then the waitress came and served them their meals. "Need anything else?" she inquired.

Grace replied, "No, everything looks fine and delicious. Thank you."

David had regained his excitement and said enthusiastically, "I know this is something you are going to thoroughly enjoy! It involves high school age students. We will create a group called, Sing HIS Praises!. We will accept every young person who wants to be part of it regardless of their ability to sing."

"Wait a minute, David," Grace interrupted with a confused expression. "Then this isn't going to be a choir or a group which would entertain. It is getting together regularly for a Hymn Sing?…Do you…"

David quickly interrupted, "No,No…We're going to entertain!"

"But David—" she started to speak with a tinge of exasperation…

Let me explain." David quickly said, "First, we will create a choir. They will do the main singing. A lot of hymns have a refrain and that's where the remaining group can join in and sing and possibly sing one or two refrains by themselves. It will all depend on the size of the group. Of course, you will sing at least two solos. That alone makes it a successful performance! We will visit convalescent homes, possibly hospitals, and maybe be able to persuade some churches or town halls to sponsor a performance. Of course there would be no admission fee. Anyway, we have one purpose here -to sing His praises to as many people as possible. What do you think?"

"It's a little mind-boggling David. I'm assuming you plan to use our churches to recruit the members and provide the practice area. I must admit I'm a bit hesitant about having everyone be accepted when we are going public to perform."

"I know Grace…but haven't you listened to a congregation singing?" He hesitated, "They don't sound too bad…Anyway, it really bothers me to tell anyone they're not good enough….

especially under circumstances such as this. We are not putting together a professional performance for payment. That would be different." He paused and gazed at her with a pleading expression that would take a strong hard-hearted person to refuse.

"Alright," she conceded, "We can give it a try with our pastors' permission."

"Thanks! You'll see—it's going to be a success."

They had finished their meal and the waitress came to see if they wanted any dessert as she cleared the table.

Grace ordered cheese cake and David apple pie.

"Well, David, if this idea of yours doesn't work with the young people, we could consider making it a duo. You and I could go about and sing His praises. I think we make a pretty good duet."

"That's a great idea! I'll hold you to it!" he answered emphatically.

The waitress brought their desserts which they both thoroughly enjoyed.

They were walking towards the car when David noticed a paper had been placed under the driver's side of the windshield wiper. A very uneasy feeling came over him and he hurried slightly so he would arrive at the car before Grace. He quickly reached out and removed the paper, folding it up to fit in his pocket.

Grace asked, "Was there something under your windshield wiper?"

"Just a flyer for some upcoming event no doubt."

"Oh, yes, I get them also."

David saw Grace safely home.

Anxious to see what the paper was he quickly pulled off the road as soon as possible. He put the light on inside the car and took the paper out of his pocket. He hesitated a moment before opening it up.

The printing had the appearance as if it had been written by a young child.

"Did you think I'd forgotten You?
Not a chance—I'm not through—
I'll continue to keep you in my sight-
Until I set things right!!

Immediately the thought went through his mind—*Someone had to be watching and following me to have put this on my car at the diner. The final words insinuate I have done something to anger them. As hard as I think into my past and present I don't have an inkling of what or whom it could be. I guess I just have to be on guard.*

CHAPTER 12

July 1950 Continued

Dear Mom and Family,

Looks like another hot July day. Rick and I are planning on doing a few chores for the landlord. They are both on in years and some tasks are too difficult for them. Neither of us want to see them paying for services that we can help with. Rick has been really great in making time to pitch in, inspite of his two jobs. We come out ahead of the deal—A home-cooked meal along with a pleasant, relaxing evening. I don't remember telling you what degree Rick is studying for—He plans to be a Primary Teacher. He likes the younger children and also feels that it is important they are exposed to a male teacher during their beginning years. It's true when I think back to elementary school I can only recall having one male teacher. However, had quite a few through High School. He will be graduating next June. I convinced him to stay another year in the apartment until he is able to finalize where he will need to be living. It will depend on where he is employed.

Summer courses are going along well. Just wish I had more free hours. Grace and I have started a teenage group called, Sing HIS Praises. We had a really good turnout at our first meeting and practice. Plan to sing at Grace's church this coming Sunday and my church the following Sunday. If these two performances are successful, then we will go to other facilities with faith that our voices will inspire many others to—Sing HIS Praises! We are blessed that several parents from both churches have volunteered their help, especially with transportation. I'll keep you posted how it turns out.

Guess it's time for me to get this day underway!

Thinking of you always.

Love,
David

David's morning class had ended in perfect time to surprise Gertrude and take her out for lunch. She was thrilled with the unexpected outing. They had returned home, played some Scrabble, visited briefly and enjoyed a treat of her homemade cookies. They finalized their time together with the pleasure of dancing to the records of the memorable music of her day. It always touched David's heart as he saw the joy and comfort that this music and dance brought to her.

He headed home in hopes of getting some of the morning's assignments done before his next class. He was making fairly good progress when Pete called him.

"David, we've got things set up for the inspection of the tenements and decided we want you to participate. This will be an unscheduled inspection for Milano's buildings only. We want to catch him and the super off-guard. It shouldn't cause any suspicion as building inspectors do this occasionally.

However you must be careful that you don't inadvertently mention it to anyone."

"I will be glad to help. When is it and what do you want me to do?" David was praying it wouldn't be during one of his classes. If it was, he would just have to miss class. This was too important not to help out.

"It's going to be this coming Thursday at approximately 10:00 A.M... We will start in Milano's Building One, at the super's office. It would be great if you could enter the building when we first start. We are anxious to observe the super's reaction when he sees you. Hopefully there will be a distance between the two of you causing him to raise his voice when he questions your reason for entering the building. The main purpose of the confrontation is to help confirm that it <u>was</u> his voice you heard on the night of the attack. There will be three of us. A detective from the police department posing as a building inspector, an accredited building inspector, and myself representing the insurance company. The detective and I will be wired. We feel that if we have substantial evidence to arrest the super, then he will give us the name of the person responsible for ordering the attack. Hopefully it will bring us one step closer in our investigation of the suspicious occurrences to Reardon's building, which is pressuring him to sell. You must make this look like an accidental meeting. Any questions?"

"I have just one question. Is it essential in which building this takes place? I have a small radio I'm taking to a friend from the Soup Kitchen who lives in the fourth building. This way when I enter the building I have a legitimate reason. I can park my car a distance from the apartments and walk to the coffee shop across the street from them. I'll get a cup of coffee and sit at one of the tables looking out toward the buildings. I'll make sure I'm at angle so I won't be visible. I will, however, be able to see and keep track of your progress since you will have to leave each building to get to the next. When you enter the last building, slowly inspect the ground floor or stop on the stairs checking the banister or the stairs themselves. This will give me time to get to the building and enter creating an appropriate distance for the confrontation."

Pete replied enthusiastically, "It doesn't matter which building. What you just suggested will be perfect! We will probably be on the ground floor because each building has the maintenance and storage closet located there. We can extend our inspection giving you ample time. I guess it's settled then. Any other questions?"…He paused slightly and added as an after-thought, "I hope this doesn't interfere with your classes."

"No it's fine. Thank you for caring."…David hesitated and then continued expressing a great deal of concern. "Do you <u>really</u> think this guy will break down and give you the information? To me the evidence against him still seems kind of weak."

"We will be taking in his entire body reaction and comments. We will interrogate him pointing out some of his options for the situation he is in. Your confirming he was involved in the attack constitutes a crime of assault." Pete concluded emphatically, "David stick to the plan! We want to keep you safe. See you Thursday. Thanks for the assistance," thus ending the conversation.

*****

David left his apartment extra early onThursday morning allowing time for any unexpected delays. He succeeded in getting the car parked and himself settled in the coffee shop before the inspection started thus ensuring he would not be seen.

Pete and his colleagues had completed their inspection of the first two buildings and were now heading toward the last one. Pete took a quick glance across the street at the coffee shop and he was relieved that he could not see David. He had no doubt, however, that David was there watching.

They entered the building and headed for the storage closet. The super, however, went to the stairs commenting, "Why waste time examining another storage closet? It's the same as all the rest! Let's get on with this and get it done. I have work to do!"

The official Building Inspector replied as he and the others continued in the direction of the closet, "Sorry, but all maintenance storage closets of each building must be examined."

The super was muttering as he followed them fumbling with his keys. They had reached the door and were waiting for him to open it.

"I can't find the key," he said in annoyance.

Just then, David entered.

The Super looked up and shouted, "What are you doing here?! I told you once, no soliciting. How many times do I have to tell you?"

"I'm just delivering a small radio to a friend in the building," David answered politely and then added on, "How many times do I have to tell you I wasn't soliciting?"

Angrily the super replied, "Make your delivery! Then leave and don't come back!"

David pondering said, "Come back?" He paused slightly and continued, "I've heard those two words before in the same familiar voice, and it wasn't in a building!"

Now the super was getting agitated and nervous and without thinking replied, "Well it wasn't me. I was out of town!"

David quickly responded, "Really. When was that?"

"June 27th visiting family, and it's none of your business.!"

David did not respond, but smiled to himself in satisfaction and thought, *the date of the mugging.* He started up the stairs to deliver the radio but stopped keeping out of sight, as an argument had occurred between the super and the inspectors. He became concerned. Maybe he should have kept his mouth shut. He moved a few steps closer and listened.

"I must have accidentally left the key on my desk when I was rearranging them. Why are we wasting time on this? Everything is the same in all the storage closets!" he said in a very provoked tone.

The Building Inspector replied, "As I told you before-All storage and maintenance closets are required to be inspected! I'm sorry, but you will have to go back and get the key."

The super replied in annoyance, "O.K., Fine! I'll go back and get the key. It shouldn't take me long."

The argument was extended as he was told that one of them would go back with him.

When David heard this he quickly put the radio down next to the wall in the hallway. He went back down the stairs as quickly as he could without drawing attention to himself as they continued to argue. As soon as he was outside he started to run. He cut down the first alley he came to between the buildings. He wanted to get off the street so he wouldn't be seen when the super was returning to his office. The alley took him to the adjoining back yards where the wash lines were strung from an apartment window to a tall sturdy pole. He got to building one where the Super's office was and found a spot out of sight where he could keep watch on the building. He stood a few minutes catching his breath and then chuckled to himself as he thought, *This is probably just a fool's errand –I reacted to the first thing that came to mind. No need to tell anyone if it turns out I'm wrong. I'll keep this foolishness to myself.*

In the meantime it had been decided that the building inspector, who was really the police detective, would walk back with the super to get the key. The super was still angry and annoyed, but calmed down as they walked.

The detective nonchalantly commented, "I guess you have to get in and out of these closets quite frequently."

"Yeah, every day! That's one of the reasons for a closet in every building with the same necessary supplies and equipment. Can't be carrying stuff from building to building."

The Super's intention was to reinforce the fact and reason for each storage closet to have the exact same supplies and thereby making it not necessary to inspect them all.

However, the detective was verifying that the super on a daily basis opened these closets and thereby would be aware of any missing or added items in them. Now he had this on tape.

Once they entered the building, the super unexpectedly shot forward practically running to his apartment. He unlocked his door and quickly entered shutting the door behind him. He shouted, "I'll go check my desk and see if the key is there, I'll be right out!"

The police detective close on the heels of the super reached the door just in time to have it shut in his face. He attempted to open it, but it was locked. "Open the door!" he demanded.

The Super responded shouting from inside, "Oh! I'm sorry! Did the door lock? I'm practically to my office so I will continue to go and check my desk. Shouldn't take me long."

Even though the super's action had been unforeseen and he had moved so quickly, the detective was annoyed with himself for letting him get out of his sight. He shouted once again, "Come and open the door!"

The super called back, "It's not on the desk! It's probably on the floor."

Now the super's voice was fading a bit.

The detective wasn't quite sure what to do. *Was locking himself into the room an accident or on purpose?…was he really looking for the key? …Or getting a weapon to over-take me since he believed me to be a building inspector and therefore I would not be armed. But what would he gain by that?….Secure me out of the room and then he could…That's it! ESCAPE… "OH, NO!"* he shouted and dashed out of the building and ran to the alley and down it.

He heard some shuffling noises followed by David's appearance with the super in tow.

"Look who I found coming out of a window?' David called.

"That's very interesting," the detective replied.

The super was struggling to free himself and shouting at David, "I'll have you arrested for this! There's no law against a man climbing out of his window. You had no right to attack me and hold me prisoner!"

When they were face to face, the detective looked at David with a twinge of amazement and asked, "How come you were here?"

"I heard some of the argument regarding the closet and that he would have to go back and get the key. So, it was just a hunch," David replied nonchalantly.

The detective just shook his head and raised his eyebrows in disbelief. He then turned his attention to the super. Showing him his badge he said, "Settle down. We are now going back calmly to see what is in that closet that you don't want discovered. I am certain you have the key. I advise you to make the trip back without causing any discord. I am armed. Shall we go?"

The super realized he had no alternative but to comply. David had a strong grip on his upper arm and he knew the detective would follow through on his warning.

The police detective had taken charge over the situation. They had joined with the remainder of their group and were standing in front of the closet in question. The detective put his hand out towards the super and stated, "Give me the key. There is nothing to gain by withholding it any longer."

The super reluctantly handed him his keys by separating the closet key from the rest.

Taking the key the detective asked, "Now, as I understand it, you have the only key to this closet. Is that correct?"

"No. There's a duplicate key in Milano's safe."

It was obvious this did not please the detective. He quickly pulled out his Handie-Talkie, which was a small lightweight two-way radio the police used to communicate. As soon as contact was made, he gave his orders, "Get a warrant as quick as you can to inspect Milano's office for the key to a maintenance closet in building 4. Check the safe first! If it's not there then continue checking the office and it's best not to let Milano know what you are looking for. It's very important you locate that key in his office before he finds out we have inspected that closet."

Slipping his radio back into his pocket, he turned towards the closet and said, "Now, let's see what the hidden treasure is!"

He unlocked the door and opened it switching on the light. The first thing that caught their attention was a gasoline can which, upon testing, proved to be full. A serious violation! However, searching to the back of the closet and almost hidden were smoke bombs.

The detective immediately asked, "What maintenance upkeep or repairs use these?"

The super remained silent.

The detective once again pulled out his radio and gave further orders. "I need a car to transport a suspect and an investigating team to gather prints and evidence. Keep this under wraps at this time."

He then took out his handcuffs and told the super his rights as he cuffed him.

The super was wise enough to keep silent, waiting until he had a lawyer to represent him.

Within a short time the police car for transporting the suspect arrived as well as the investigating team who immediately got to work setting up barriers around the closet area.

The detective thanked Pete and the accredited building inspector for their help. He turned to David and said, "That was very clever of you to get the super to actually say the date of the mugging in an attempt to defend himself. It's perfect, as we now have this on tape. Only those involved in that confrontation would know that date and what you were referring to. It wasn't publicized. We also had spoken with the resident who did not completely shut his door when the super confronted you in the hall. He had heard the conversation with reference to the curious cat where 'satisfaction' brought it back. This coincided with the mugger's comment that 'no satisfaction would bring you back'. I still can't get over your quick analyzing that the super was planning his escape through the window and your getting there in time to catch him. I wonder have you ever given thought to the profession of police investigator? You seem to have the qualifications."

"It was just a lucky assumption. I can assure you. That is not a profession I'm interested in. Thanks anyway for the compliment. Glad I could help. Good luck with your suspect."

"I best get my suspect to the station. I'm glad I had the opportunity to meet you. I will keep you informed. Don't discuss this episode with anyone as yet. Be careful, David."

As Pete and David were about to leave the building, David asked, "Why is it so important that a key to this closet is found in Milano's office?"

"Because without a key to that closet the guilt of the smoke bombs and gasoline falls completely on the super! There's no other way to go. Milano having a key, which he keeps hidden in a locked safe, makes him a viable suspect as well. Why would the owner of a building keep the only other key to a specific maintenance storage room, or to any storage room, for that matter? That in itself raises a great deal of suspicion. The bottom line is—the key connects him to the illegal items in a building he owns. It gives the authorities a feasible reason to pursue investigating him."

"Wow! I didn't realize how complicated things can get. Thanks again, Pete. I'm glad I got the chance to meet you."

"Same here! Take care David and I'll be in touch."

They left the building each going to tend to the needs of their day!

*****

David heaved a sigh and was glad this day was over. He was heading to his bedroom when the phone rang.

He reluctantly picked it up, not eager for a phone call at this time of night. "Hello, this is David." He didn't recognize the voice which immediately starting speaking. "WHAT" David shouted just as he heard the click ending the call.

David stood there stupefied, staring at the phone in his hand. He finally managed to utter—"You've got to be kidding!"

CHAPTER 13

August 1950

Dear Mom and Family,

I can't believe it's the first of August! Before I know it, I'll be facing finals thus ending my summer semester. I'll be back to a heavy schedule come September.

I don't remember if I told you, but Grace placed first in her test for a Certified Insurance Underwriter. Didn't surprise me! I was sure she would ace it! This puts her in line for the position when it becomes available. I know she's pleased with the results but I know it's not what she really wants to be doing. I'll have to give this some serious thought. There must be some way she could quit and pursue her desire to teach vocal music.

Our group, Sing His Praises, has been a great success! We have several performances scheduled. Two churches plus a community organization. The young people involved demonstrate an overwhelming enthusiasm and are thoroughly enjoying it! Several parents providing transportation also are feeling the powerful affect of praising God through singing, regardless of ability.

Guess that about sums things up.

I pray this finds all of you in good health and enjoying the warmth and beauty of the season. Miss you!

Love,
David

It was a little before 5:00 a.m. when Rick arrived home having completed his overnight shift. He noticed David putting the letter into the envelope and commented, "Hey, David. looks like you've been up for awhile. Got coffee made and appears you've completed your letter as well. Have some assignments to catch up on too?"

"No. I woke up and couldn't get back to sleep. Decided I might just as well do something useful rather than just lying in bed thinking."

As Rick opened the refrigerator to get some orange juice, he glanced back at David. Something wasn't right. David appeared deep in thought but more than that he definitely was disturbed. He walked over to the table, his juice in hand, and asked, "We're friends. Right David?"

The question made David quickly look up at Rick and ask in disbelief, "Why in the world are you asking me that? Of course we are!"

"That's what I thought." Rick pulled out a chair and sat down at the table across from David. "So, what's wrong? That's part of friendship, you know, sharing and being there for each other." He paused, and then said, "I'm listening."

David hesitated briefly as though trying to find the words. Finally he said, "I received a weird call last night. The voice was not familiar. They probably dialed a wrong number and it wasn't meant for me. It bothers me that someone might be in danger and I can't do anything about it."

Rick looked across the table directly at David and said, "It must be a whopper of a message causing you to go into denial. So tell me…what was it?"

"I'm not in deni…" David stopped and then went on to say, "O.K. I suppose it could be for me. It just doesn't make any sense… See what you can make out of it." David took a deep breath and said—here it is, "Change your profession and I might let you live."

"Wow! That is weird. I can't think of anything in your choice of profession that could cause that kind of a threat!" He sighed and continued, "David, you've put it off long enough. You need to report to the police all of these messages and the previous incidences in which you could have been seriously injured or worse. I'm urging you to do this as a friend who cares about you!"

"Rick, as I've told you before…I do not have any substantial evidence to support that those incidences were definitely connected. Since I was so involved trying to keep control of the car, I am unable to give any identifying facts regarding cars or people involved. Also, in some of the incidences there wasn't any person or car visible. The police have nothing to work with. If this person really wants me dead, he or she would have succeeded by now. I believe their real intention is to intimidate me…for what reason?—I don't have a fathom of an idea."

Rick thought, *I don't agree with you. Their efforts to injure or kill you just didn't succeed due to circumstances.* But instead…. he answered, "O.K. What you just said makes some sense except there is one thing you overlooked. The two notes you received. There could be some identifying information on them that the police may be able to discern. I know you still have them." The next sentence was said with profound emotion, "I'm asking you to please turn them over to the police on the chance of their finding a lead to the person or persons responsible for the threats."

David looked across the table at his concerned friend, "O.K. Rick. I'll take them in today. It's kinda late to be turning them in but I will explain."

Rick replied with a sincere, "Thanks!"

"You've put in a long night of work. I think it's time you headed for bed."

"Yeah, I guess I am a little tired. I have to admit, our conversation was quite stimulating," Rick said as he got up from the table and rinsed his juice glass at the sink. "But I think I'm ready for some shuteye."

Just as he was closing his bedroom door he heard David say, "Thanks friend. Sleep well."

David sat at the table for a few minutes longer and then decided he might just as well take his shower and get ready to start his day. He decided to stop at the diner for breakfast as he wasn't in the mood to prepare anything. Just before leaving he reluctantly got the two flyers to take to the police as he had told Rick he would.

Feeling somewhat better after having a proper breakfast he headed for the police station. *Might as well get this over with. Since it has been quite a long time they may not care to be bothered with it.* He entered the station and went to the front desk. He explained about the flyers and his request for their inspection in hopes of possibly getting a lead.

The officer asked him, "With the exception of yourself, has anyone else handled these?

"No. As soon as I read them, I slipped them into the plastic bags to avoid that from happening."

"You waited quite awhile before bringing them in. Any special reason for that?"

"No. I was just shrugging them off as a prank."

"And…what changed your mind?"

David sighed…he really didn't want to go into too much detail. "A friend of mine kept badgering me, so I gave in."

"Wise friend," he commented and slipped a form and pen across the counter to David. "Fill this out with your information and we'll see what we can find out. We will be in touch with you as soon as the tests are completed."

David complied and as he handed the completed form back to the officer he said, "Thanks. I appreciate this."

"No problem. Have a good day and keep your eyes open for anything suspicious and report it to us."

"Will do," David answered as he left the station thinking, *I guess Rick was on the money as the saying goes. He was right to have me bring these in. Sure surprised me of the officer's concern. I figured they wouldn't take the threats that seriously as I imagine they must get a good number of bogus notes. I guess though they can't take the chance that one is real and the person is in danger.*

*****

It was Saturday and Sing His Praises had just finished their performance sponsored by a church on the outskirts of Eagerton. It was well attended and joyfully received. The church members had prepared refreshments for the group. Grace and David were watching the teenagers mingling and enjoying this time together. They were close enough to the food table to hear Alma exclaim in a raised voice of annoyance and disappointment, "You took the last chocolate cupcake which is my favorite!" The accusation was directed at Saundra who was just about to place the cupcake on her plate. Saundra, however, reached over and put it on Alma's plate and took one of the remaining vanilla cupcakes from the serving tray. Alma did not acknowledge the unselfish gift, but just turned and walked away in a huff with her treasure as if it were due her.

David and Grace were stunned by Alma's behavior. Saundra, on the other hand, showed no inkling of surprise at the response nor regret for giving up her chocolate cupcake to the ungrateful Alma.

Grace stopped Saundra as she was walking past and said, "That was a very caring and unselfish thing you just did. I have the feeling that Alma's reaction was not a surprise to you."

"No, it wasn't. I don't know why, but she has always disliked me. It doesn't help that I don't have a very good singing voice. She resents those of us who don't sing well being part of the group."

"I would guess that chocolate is your favorite as well? Yet you gave it away to someone who is mean to you?"

"I'm just trying to follow Jesus' teaching in Matthew 5:39 where He tells us "that if anyone slaps us on the right cheek, turn to them the other cheek also". When I was younger I always thought of this as a physical hurt. Now that I'm older and more aware of emotional hurt as well, I think Jesus meant both kinds of hurt. So I am just turning the other cheek.

You know what? Alma's actions and comments don't hurt anymore. I feel sorry for her and hope she changes and stops looking down at others who aren't as privileged as she is."

Grace was deeply touched by this profound answer from the teenager. She thought, *sometimes we really do sell our teenagers short.* Grace replied, "Alma, thank you for sharing that with me. Ultimately, by showing love and concern to those who are on the wrong path always results in our receiving God's blessings."

When the social time ended, the teenagers in need of a ride home went to their respective drivers. Several rode with David and Grace.

David having dropped off his last passenger asked Grace, "Do you have any plans for the rest of the day?"

"Just house-cleaning."

"That's a terrible way to spend the rest of the afternoon! Could I interest you in joining me on a home-visit to one of the parishioners of my church? I know he would greatly enjoy meeting you."

"That definitely sounds much more intriguing!"

On the way to Harry's residence, David filled Grace in on Harry's disability. He also warned her of the possibility that Harry might act annoyed by their visit. He advised her to just ignore it.

They were now at Harry's door and just before David knocked he looked at Grace and said, "Be prepared."

The door opened and they were greeted with a slight tone of annoyance, "Oh, it's you!" followed by, "and you brought company." He wheeled his chair out of the way and said gruffly, "Well, come on in."

David introduced Grace and to his surprise, Harry reached out and shook her hand saying, "Pleased to meet you."

"My pleasure as well. I'm glad David invited me to come."

"Let's go sit in the living room. It will be more comfortable than these kitchen chairs," he said as he lead the way. When they entered the room, Grace noticed some of his paintings, but did not get the chance to look at them all. Harry had immediately guided her to a chair. Once they were all settled and had enjoyed some casual conversation, Harry asked David what the Bible study was for their get-together.

David answered, "I thought each of us might like to choose one of their favorite scriptures and share the reason for the choice. A good chance each of us might add to our own list. However, if either of you have a preferred Bible study, please say so."

They were all in agreement to David's suggestion which by the sharing of the readings did result in an open discussion involving their many emotions and situations they were faced with everyday.

Following the study they had an extended hymn sing. Harry joined in with several of the hymns, but he preferred to listen to the melodious voices of Grace and David.

They were getting ready to leave, when Grace expressed the desire to look more closely at Harry's paintings as well as the ones she hadn't seen. She came upon one that caused her to gasp, bringing her hand to her mouth as she stood gazing at it as if hypnotized.

Seeing her reaction Harry and David became concerned.

David immediately walked over to her and asked in a lowered and worried voice, "Are you O.K.?" as he glanced up at the picture.

The painting which held her captive was of a small cottage surrounded by flowers. A large farm house and barn stood a short distance away further back from the cottage. There were cows grazing in a field in the distance. Her attention, however was drawn to the small vegetable garden near the cottage where a woman and a child were tending to it.

"Yes. I'm alright," she softly answered David as she tried to gain control of her emotions. She turned and asked Harry, "Did you know the people who owned this farm?"

"No. Often when I finished a painting and did not have anything special in my mind to paint next, I would go for a drive. As soon as I came upon that cottage and saw the woman and the child working in the garden and laughing together…" He then said emphatically, "I knew it was my next painting! I took several pictures at different angles and used them as my guide."

"Would you consider selling this painting?" She hesitated, then continued in a slightly broken voice, "You see, the woman is my mother and the child is me. I lived in that cottage until I was 12 years old." Overcome with emotion, she had to pause…. "They were the happiest years of my life!"

Now it was Harry and David who were stunned and left speechless for a few moments.

Harry broke the silence when he said in a strong authoritative voice. "David take that painting down and give it to this lovely young lady. Please replace it with any of the canvasses leaning against the wall. Thank you."

He now said to Grace, "This is my gift to you in return for the priceless gift you have given me."

Grace was confused, and answered, "I haven't given you any gift. Please let…"

Before Grace could finish her sentence, Harry interrupted, "I cannot describe how deeply it touches me to know that I have created something that brings such fond memories to the heart of another person. That is the gift you have given me."

Grace understood and conceded saying sincerely, "Thank You for this precious gift."

David carried her painting as they made their way to the kitchen in preparation of leaving.

Harry reached up and shook David's hand as well as Grace's and said, "Thank you for the visit. You are always welcome."

With that most unexpected invitation they left with a happy warm feeling.

David had planned to invite Grace to dinner, but under the circumstances he wasn't sure if she would prefer to go home. He really didn't want to take her home to a lonely apartment. He decided to ask her outright what her preference was. This way she could answer truthfully without feeling guilty about turning him down from his offer of dinner. Taking a depth breath, he thought, *here goes nothing, I hope it's the right decision.*

"Grace, what is your preference? Do you wish to go home or go to dinner? I fully will understand whichever choice you make."

She looked over at him and said with grateful sincerity, "Dinner with you sounds wonderful. Thank you."

It was obvious that David was pleased with her reply as his voice revealed how glad he was. "I thought of trying a new restaurant a friend of mine suggested. He guarantees me the food is like having a home cooked meal. What do you say....want to try it?"

"Yes, it sounds very intriguing."

The restaurant was small having the ambiance of a warm and cozy home. They were seated at a secluded table providing privacy. A waiter came promptly and took their order.

David noticed that Grace seemed calmer but still somewhat distressed. He sensed that the painting brought memories of happy times but along with it came sadness as well.

They sat in silence for a few minutes when David said in a calming voice, "I recall an incident when I was having a difficult time trying to sort out conflicting concerns and trying to control an annoying emotion."

He paused for a moment and continued, "A very kind and caring young woman said to me, 'I am more than willing to listen. Sometimes, just verbalizing can help.'…. I just want you to know that I'm here for you and more than willing to listen, if needed."

At that moment the waiter brought their meals. When he confirmed they were not in need of anything else, he left.

The aroma smelled enticing causing them both to be anxious to take a taste, which resulted in comments of "delicious" and "it does taste home cooked."

After a few more moments Grace said, "My parents were very poor when I was born. My father had aspirations of becoming a very successful actor, which of course, was not conducive to earning the necessary funds to support a family. Fortunately, my mother heard about the owner of this affluent farm who was looking to hire a couple. The wife, to do the housekeeping and other minor duties, while the husband helped with farm chores. Their salary would consist of their living quarters, which was the furnished cottage, plus a moderate cash sum."

Grace took a break and ate some of her meal. David did not make any comments, he just listened intently.

"Through the first few years my father held up his part of the agreement, with only missing several days by going to auditions. My mother filled in on those days and did some of his chores that she was capable of and received payment in return, so they did not lose the whole day's pay. Of course she still had to meet all of her own responsibilities. They needed every bit of the cash to purchase the necessary items such as food, clothing, etc." Grace sighed, took another bite of food and looked up at David and said, "Are you bored yet?"

David quickly replied, "No, not at all! I'm interested in knowing everything about you and your life…Just make sure you eat your meal before it gets cold."

"I am and it's delicious!" After a few more bites, she continued, "My mother took me with her to the big house in my pre-school years. She always made sure I had things to occupy me as she did her work. Once I started school, then when I came home I would go to the cottage first to see if Mom was there.

If she wasn't I would go to the big house and help her with dusting, or sweeping or with whatever chore I was capable of doing. She always found ways to make it fun. My favorite was when she pretended to be the mean sister and I was Cinderella. Sometimes we would choose a chore and see who would finish first and that person would get an extra cookie when we got home." She gave a yearning sigh.

David tensed up a bit as he was aware of a slight change in Grace's voice. He perceived she was now coming to the reason that caused her emotional distress.

"My father seemed to be away more than at home. This put more pressure on my mother but she never changed her sense of fun and joy for the life she was given. We talked, sang and laughed as we went through all our busy days. Then when I was twelve, one day without warning she had an aneurysm of the brain. She died quickly and did not suffer."

David with unabashed tears in his eyes reached over and took hold of Grace's hand and said compassionately, "I'm so sorry, Grace."

She nodded in acknowledgement and appreciation for his obvious sharing of the pain she felt.

The waiter came and cleared the table of their dishes and offered a choice of dessert. They both ordered a chocolate brownie with ice cream.

Grace continued, "The funeral consisted only of the immediate family. When we got back to the cottage, my father told me to go to my room and start gathering my clothing and any other personal things I had. I knew we couldn't stay at the cottage, but I didn't expect to have to leave this soon. I heard my aunt raising her voice as she said, 'You can't do this!' Obviously spoken to my father. I opened my door a crack and listened. I can hear the words today as clearly as I did then. My father was talking, "This is a great opportunity and I cannot pass it by. Before Hope died she emphatically agreed that I should go. As soon as I'm settled in California with my part in the movie I will come and get Grace."

My aunt replied in angry sarcasm, "As soon as you get the part! How many sure auditions have you gone to and you were not selected?" Now, forcefully my aunt continued, "I guarantee you, Fred, Hope certainly does not want you to abandon Grace at this time! You need to put aside this overwhelming desire to act and take on the responsibility of being a father! When Grace is grown, then do whatever you want!"

My father replied in a pleading voice, "She is almost a teenager. She needs a mother more than a father. I'm only asking you to take care of her for 2 months. Living with you and her cousins will probably help her to get over the loss of her mother quicker than her being alone while I work. I just don't have the time for her right now! I can't miss this audition!"

My aunt sighed and said relenting, "You might be right. Grace is more than welcome into my home and her cousins would love having her. You promise to come for her in two months, acting job or not. Agreed?"

"Yes, yes! I will also write to her keeping her informed of how things are going and she can write back as soon as I'm settled."

Grace looked directly at David and said, "I shut the door and went about gathering my stuff up. I doubted my father would ever come for me."

The waiter delivered their dessert and made sure they didn't want anything else. He totaled the bill, put it on the table and left.

David did not want to ask, as he felt fairly certain Grace's father did not return to get her.

Grace looked up at David and said in earnest, "I have never told anyone about my life, as I didn't feel capable to. Thank you, David. You made it possible for me to be able to cherish the happy memories of my mother without it being shadowed by the sadness of the abandonment of my father. Your sincere concern made it easy for me to tell you of my youth and in so doing, I came to the realization that my father never showed any real caring or love to my mother or me. He had, in a sense, abandoned us long before my mother's death. So God provided for me a loving home with my Aunt and Uncle and cousins until I could take care of myself."

David was still holding Grace's hand gently from the time she told him of her mother's death. His hold tightened slightly as he looked up at her with tenderness and a yearning to hold her in his arms to offer more comfort. He did sense, however, that she seemed to have a peace within herself and she would now be able to thoroughly enjoy Harry's painting. Now when she looked at it, she would only feel the happy memories she carried within her heart as well as the comfort of knowing her mother was now home with her Savior.

*****

Several days later, David was just about to sit down to eat his supper and study for up-coming finals when the phone rang. In spite of himself, he couldn't always control the apprehension he felt prior to picking up the phone.

"Greetings, this is David."

"David, this is the Pastor. I'm glad I reached you. I have a favor to ask. Would you be free this coming Friday from 8:30 to Noon or any time you could give between those hours?"

"I can help to 11:00. I have an 11:30 class. What do you need done?"

"You'd better sit down when I tell you this."

David chuckled, "I think I'm O.K. Go ahead and tell me."

"I need help in setting up Harry's paintings at the Eagerton Gallery."

What?!" David exclaimed.

The pastor laughed and asked, "Now are you sitting down or did you faint?"

"I'm speechless! That's what I am!" David then continued in disbelief, "He really is going to do a showing and sell his paintings? That's wonderful! Do you know what changed his mind?"

"Yes, I do. It seems someone visited him and made him realize the power an artist has in capturing on canvas pictures that touch the hearts, and memories, of people and also transport people to places they dream about but can't go. He also added they can capture God's beautiful gifts of nature—tranquil lakes, flowers, sunrises and sunsets, birds, animals—there's no end to his list! David, he now knows why God doesn't come and take him! He sees the purpose of his life! He is gratefully accepting help and willing to go out of the apartment."

David was amazed, but managed to say, "I'll be there at eight."

He hung the phone up and stood in silence for a moment and then sent a heartfelt prayer of "Thanks."

Next, he said aloud and excitedly, "I've got to call Grace!" He immediately picked up the phone.

Having completed his call to Grace, who was just as excited as he was, he returned to his supper and his plans to study. However, he hardly got settled when the phone rang again. He sighed and got up and answered it.

"Hey David, this is Pete!" There was no doubt he was excited about something.

"What's got you so excited?" David inquired.

"Tomorrow be outside of the police station around 1:00 pm. Grace will be there also. She made arrangements to change her lunch time."

"What's going on? That's a strange place to ask me to be as well as Grace?"

Pete answered emphatically, "Just be there!" and hung up. He had a habit of doing that—leaving a person in the dark.

David shook his head bewildered as he hung the phone up. Once again he spoke aloud, "Why in the world would I want to be outside of the police station?!"

He looked over at his supper and books and thought, *Guess I'll give it another try. I'm getting hungry. However, it's going to be difficult to concentrate on studying.* As he sat down at the table, he mumbled, "Outside of the police station—Only Pete would make that kind of a request!"

CHAPTER 14

August 1950 Continued

Dear Mom and Family,

Just wanted to drop you a short line to let you know all is well.

Sing His Praises has made quite a hit and we have several more performances scheduled. We plan to have them perform at the Soup Kitchen. I know they will be warmly received and it will be a good experience for them as well.

I'm still working on a plan to help Grace to be able to pursue her dream of teaching vocal music.

I seem to be so short of time these days. I really need to make time for preparing for the up-coming finals. They'll be here before I

*know it! Looking forward to the short break
before the fall semester.*

> *Guess that's about it. Keeping you all in
my prayers.*

*Love,
David*

David arrived at the police station ahead of the appointed time. He surveyed the area and everything appeared normal with one exception. He was sure there were a couple of newspaper reporters with their cameras, lingering about rather inconspicuously.

Grace arrived and came over to him and asked, "Do you know what this is all about?"

David answered, "Not a clue. You know Pete— he enjoys keeping people in suspense."

Grace laughed. "That he does! I do think though that he is always on guard for fear of letting something become known that is best kept under wraps, because he is the Insurance Company's Investigator."

"Possibly—but this is pretty public out here."

Pete came out of the police station and as he walked over to them he said, "Glad you made it! Just have a few minutes more to wait."

He no sooner finished the sentence when a police car pulled up to the curb. Both officers got out. One went to the back door of the car, while the other stood by on guard.

David had been right—the reporters were now positioned to get their pictures.

The policeman opened the back door of the car and assisted the hand-cuffed prisoner out.

Pete said with extreme satisfaction, "That man is Mr. Milano, who previously was known as Mr.Erick Sanderson, owner of the tenement building that burned down from my previous employment."

Grace and David had never come face to face, nor saw any pictures of Milano. They only knew him by name.

The cameras flashed!

Milano's expression was arrogant with no signs of regret for the lives he had taken nor the plans to burn down four more occupied tenement buildings. Money was all he thought about!

David was aware he had a temper which he didn't always succeed at keeping in complete control. He always was, however, capable of restraining from retaliating in a physical manner because that was not his nature.

BUT—He had never felt this kind of anger that soared up within him along with the desire to attack this man -AS HE DID NOW!

Pete sensed it, and took hold of David's arm and said softly, "Get a hold of yourself. I don't need an assault charge against you!"

He also heard Grace's soft voice say, "Vengeance is mine, saith the Lord."

Ironically, the police walked Milano in front of David as they made their way into the building. Grace's words had given David the control he needed as he prayed and released the strong desire, turning the matter over to the Lord.

Pete faced David and said, "I'm sorry. I had no idea that seeing Milano would affect you that strongly. I wanted you to have the full satisfaction of seeing him in custody, especially since you were the reason for it happening."

"What are you talking about? You're the one who has never given up and continued pursuing him."

"That is true, but you are the one who was clever enough to make the super admit on tape that he knew about the assault and confirmed the date. You also stopped him from making his escape! In order to save himself from more detrimental charges, he told us everything. This gave the FBI the power to open up files that revealed that Erick Sanderson had changed his name and all other identification to Hendrik Milano. That's why I kept hitting dead ends when I was trying to track down Sanderson. By the way, the purpose of the smoke bombs was to encourage the residents to leave the building prior to igniting the fire, thereby hopefully averting injury or death.

Looking David straight in the eye he said more emphatically, "Sanderson/Milano, whatever you want to call him by, will never know what freedom is again. We have him on multiple murder charges as well as premeditated arson of 4 occupied tenement buildings. Thank you, David, for putting your life on the line as well as saving lives. I'm sure Milano was beginning to seriously think of permanently getting rid of you."

*****

It was Sunday evening at the Soup Kitchen and most of the people had left with the exception of a few who were still eating. The workers decided to have a snack break before cleaning up. They also did not want to make the few remaining feel as though they had to rush their meal, so they sat down at a table next to the small group.

Paul said to David, "I understand that the artist who had his showing this past Friday is a parishioner of your church. The affair certainly was successful with a great turnout and he sold many paintings. I bought one for home and one for here, which needs to be hung in the near future. It was difficult to make the choice. All of them were exquisite."

"That's something the pastor has been trying to convince him of for a long time."

One of the other helpers asked David, "Is your church the one next to the abandoned warehouse?"

"Yes. The church has use of part of the building which they use for many of their church and community services and activities."…he paused and then added with a yearning in his voice, "I wish I had the money to buy that old building."

Several chuckled at that comment and one person from the other table mumbled, "What would you do with it?"

Grace noticed that excited look that came to David's eyes whenever he had one of his ideas, or perhaps dreams, might describe it more accurately.

"It has such potential!" he said with enthusiasm.

"Potential?" one of the helpers asked incredulously.

David replied, "O.K. Follow along with me and visualize this. Since it's a warehouse most of the interior is open space—making it easy to divide it up into several areas or rooms. First of all, the church's section could be enlarged giving more room for their activities. A gym would be one of the added items. All kinds of physical activities could take place for all ages. Next, a free health clinic, to serve the surrounding community and a few pleasant rooms for counseling. One of which I would call, Find Employment. A list would be kept of all available employment opportunities to aid those seeking work. This takes care of the ground floor. Now, on the second floor would be over-night sleeping quarters including bathrooms with showers. Two separate sections one for women and one for men. The remaining space would be divided into two adequate emergency apartments for those who have family and find themselves homeless due to circumstances beyond their control. They would receive help in finding permanent living quarters."

Paul said in astonishment, "Well, you certainly have covered just about everything. However, the cost of what you have just outlined would be phenomenal!"

"Oh!" David said, "I forgot to mention, I would make the warehouse a gift to the church.

That way it would be tax exempt. We would create an extended volunteer list as well as making contact with large well-known companies for their tax deductible donations, which would consist of money, materials or labor. In return we would let the public know of their caring support. Other companies might decide to jump on the band-wagon for the publicity."

One of the others at the table expressed in deep thought, "Hmm. It might work. But you would need a lot of volunteer help!"

"True," David replied and continued saying, "We have a large number of families in this area who would benefit from all the services which this project has to offer. I'm sure many would be more than willing to give some of their time to aide in phone calls soliciting support as well as donating some of their skills and time towards the manual work."

Paul said, "David, I certainly admire all the detailed thought you have given to this project. But let's be practical. Nothing can be done until someone has the money to purchase the warehouse and that also depends on whether the owner wants to sell."

"I know," David sighed. "I tried a few weeks ago to make contact with him or her. It was to no avail. The only one I spoke with was the administrator of the property. He took my name and phone number and also told me with no hesitation that I should not expect a return call. His client was not available for any discussions relevant to the warehouse. He said, however, he would relay my request.—I just would like to speak with this person and maybe influence him in considering this project. If he didn't want to give it to the church, he could set it up as a charitable organization." David then said a little forceful, "It's standing there empty when it could be so useful! Such a waste is really irritating."

Grace could not hide her smile of admiration. She also knew David well enough to know that he would continue to pursue this project. His entire body language along with those revealing eyes implied,—I'll find a way!

Paul replied as he was getting up from the table, "I know David, there are a lot of buildings like that! Some are apartment buildings just rotting away and even a danger in some aspects.

But we can't right all the wrongs of this world David. Once you have given something your best effort and it's not successful, consider the fact that

God might have other plans for it. Remember to follow our Lord or walk with Him, but do not walk ahead of Him. So leave the matter peacefully in His hands and move on being ever aware of whatever else might come your way."

"Thank you," David replied humbly. "I admit, I do get caught up and overly excited when an idea hits me." Then he said whole-heartedly, "I really have trouble controlling it! But I will try to restrain myself in the future!"

They were now heading towards the kitchen to start working on the clean-up. Paul responded quickly to David's comment, "Oh! David! Don't lose the joy and the enthusiasm that takes hold of you!" The next comment was said in jest, "It would be denying us the fun of watching and listening to you!" He paused, and added in a concerned voice, "Just don't let frustration take over, if it doesn't succeed."

Since everyone pitched in, the Soup Kitchen and facilities were all in order within a reasonable time. Everyone left to go to whatever plans they had made for the evening.

As usual, Grace and David stopped at the diner for their evening snack.

*****

David, having completed his last final for the semester, left the college with an all consuming feeling of freedom. No more classes to attend nor home assignments to do for a couple of weeks. He stopped at the ice-cream parlor and treated himself to a chocolate marshmallow sundae before going home. He had special plans for the evening but had to wait until Grace got home from work. He hoped she didn't have any other arrangements and would accept his invitation. He did some house cleaning to help pass the time. Finally, keeping a positive attitude, he decided to shower and get ready.

He went over and picked up the phone and dialed, having difficulty to control his exhilaration for the surprise he had for her. "Hello Grace, this is David. Do you have plans for your dinner?"

"No. I just got home a little while ago."

"I took my last final today and I'm certain that I have passed them all. So, how about celebrating with me? I thought we could go to dinner at any restaurant of your choice and follow that with a drive to the park. It's such a nice evening for a stroll along the path. We could find a bench and watch the sunset. How does that sound?"

"Wonderful! I need a little time to freshen up."

"That's fine. It will take me about a half hour to get there from my apartment. The three knocks you hear at your door will be me. See you soon."

They had a delicious dinner with delightful conversation and were now enjoying their walk through the park. It was a perfect evening with a balmy breeze which relieved some of the heat from the day's sun.

Grace sensed an elated mood in David which he seemed to be trying to control. She wondered, *Was it the freedom from college classes?—or—does he have some new plan? If that is so, then without a doubt, it will include me and I may not be able to help. Well, I have something to tell him and now is as good a time as any.*

However, before she got the chance David took her gently by the elbow and ushered her to a nearby bench excitedly saying, "I have something important to tell you."

As soon as they were comfortably seated facing each other, David looked at her and said with emphatic joy, "You have an appointment this Saturday morning at 10:00 at the Morgan City Music Academy. I know they are going to interview you for their special grant that is designated for outstanding and deserving recommended applicants." He took a short breath and said with hesitation, "Of course, I can't guarantee you will be accepted." He paused and then continued with some confidence, "However, you do have one of the board members strongly in your favor!"

Grace was speechless! She wasn't sure she heard David right. *The prestigious Morgan City Academy? Impossible! But—that would certainly be having a dream come true!*

"David, I don't understand. Who knows me with that kind of status to recommend me?"

David smiled and said, "Ever since you told me of your desire to teach, I began researching for a means for you to be able to fulfill that dream. Unfortunately, all the colleges and government organizations I contacted did not have a feasible program. Then, all of a sudden I remembered a friend of mine who had mentioned his involvement with a Music Academy but I couldn't remember the name of it. I called him and when he told me Morgan City Academy I felt disappointed because I had already called there to no avail. He inquired for my concern and I told him. My friend decided to come to one of our Sing His Praises performances. He was impressed with your voice and your manner of instructing and working with the students. The latter was a very important factor and as a result, he decided to sponsor you. I would have introduced you, but he wished to remain anonymous. I just got the call late yesterday regarding the interview appointment. I wanted to be with you and in a nice quiet place when I told you. It has been most difficult keeping it to myself this long."

She affectionately gazed at David unable to speak. She didn't want him to know of the conflict this appointment caused her. She knew within her heart that he had greatly influenced his friend's decision. She was aware from experience that when David feels something very deeply within, you find yourself captive of the same emotions. The thought that she actually had a chance to be accepted by the board to get her degree in music was overwhelming!

Finally, she gained control over her conflicting emotions. She was deeply grateful to David for his persistent efforts to make her wish come true and seeing his joy compelled her to lean forward and give him a brief hug. "Thank you!" she whispered.

Looking at her fondly, David took hold of her hand and tenderly said, "Grace, if there is anyone in this world who deserves to have their dream come true—It's you. I felt that deep desire within you and I had to try to do something. It would please me if you would let me drive you to the appointment. I want to be there giving you whatever support you might need."

Grace replied, "I certainly appreciate your offer to drive. It will definitely relieve me of some of the anxiety I believe I will be feeling. However, more importantly, it will be wonderful to have your company."

He smiled and said, "My pleasure." He turned on the bench to face the view before him and commented, "Look, the sun is starting to set!...it's already beautiful."

Grace didn't reply immediately as she was still pondering her dilemma.

David glanced at her and could tell she was deep in thought and he sensed she seemed disturbed. He was concerned she was worrying about the interview and that was the last thing he wanted. This prompted him to ask, "Grace you seem a bit upset. I hope it's not due to the up-coming interview."

"No," she replied, "I...I was wondering if you have had any success with regards to the warehouse? I had the feeling you were going to still pursue it." She sighed, *What possessed me to say that?*

"No. I made one more phone call and received the same reply. I'm going to take Paul's advice and leave it in God's hands."

"That sounds like a wise decision."

She shifted in her seat to also face the ongoing panorama that only God could create.

The evening was picking up a bit of a chill with the sun slowing disappearing. David put his arm around Grace's shoulders and drew her a bit closer to him.

Grace had to admit it felt wonderful to feel his protective arm around her along with the knowledge that he truly cared about her. She decided to sort her problem out a little later. Right now she wanted to enjoy this special time together and she sensed David felt the same.

Once the sun set David took Grace home seeing her safely to her apartment.

She turned the light on as soon as she entered. It was time now to settle down and make her decision. She started to organize her thoughts. *I can't believe that when I get the unexpected opportunity to move up into the position of Insurance Underwriter with a substantial pay increase, that at the same time comes the possibility of pursuing my vocal music teaching degree! I'm obligated to give the company my answer tomorrow as to whether I wish to accept the position or not. It will go into effect this coming Monday and the person filling my position will also start Monday. There is one drawback since the position is at one of the company's branches, I will have to drive a distance to work. I will need to decide if it is financially advisable to move to the city where the branch is located.*

She sighed, *Now the real dilemma. I don't know how long a period it will be before being notified of the academy's decision. It can't be more than a few weeks due to the starting of the fall semester. If I accept the promotion and I do receive the grant, then I will be in the position only a couple of weeks at the most. These couple of weeks will be mostly getting fully adjusted to the procedures of the position. They would be wasted weeks for the company. Something about that just doesn't feel right. I could turn down the company's offer, but if I don't get the grant then I will remain in my present position until who knows when?*

She sat in silent meditation a bit longer and then prayed to God that her decision pleased Him and He would bless the outcome.

David was feeling quite happy on his way home. It had been a great evening! He knew Grace was excited about the prospects of the grant. He also sensed a deeper relationship was developing between them. He knew he cared about her a great deal and this evening she also had demonstrated a fondness towards him.

He turned into his driveway and noticed his mailbox was open. He had picked up his mail earlier and was sure he had closed the box. He stopped and as he got out of the car thought, *I guess I did't shut it all the way.* As he went to close it, he noticed he must have missed a piece of the mail. He reached in and discovered it appeared to be an advertisement. He stuffed it in his pocket, went and parked the car and headed up to the apartment. Rick had already left for work. David was about to sit in his favorite chair when he remembered the piece of paper he had stuffed in his pocket. He got up and retrieved it. It was folded in half. When he opened it up he flopped into his chair as he read the message. 'Your finals are done and that is great, Now be careful not to make a mistake, Change your profession before it's too late, To safeguard what will be your fate!'

David shook his head in exasperation and got up to get a plastic bag to put the message into.

Guess I'll drop it off at the police station some time tomorrow. Probably as always, no prints except mine.

He sat back down in his chair deep in thought. *Whomever it is seems to know a lot about my where-a bouts as well as where I live... Since I've been in Eagerton I can't think of anyone I've had a confronta- tion with... It must be someone from my past who now lives here. Still, what could cause anyone such concern as to what profession I'm preparing for? It just doesn't make any sense… This person must be unbalanced. I guess I'd best take the police warning to be on the alert. I really don't want to think what the outcome could be if these threats are carried out!*

CHAPTER 15

August 1950 Continued

Dear Mom and Family,

I have started my short break between semesters and I'm enjoying the free time. I plan to get home for a visit but not sure just when. There is a good chance that Grace may receive a grant from a music academy. It would be wonderful if this comes to fruition and she could get the degree she desires so much. The academy is quite a distance from Eagerton and she probably will have to move to Morgan City. If that is the case, then I plan on being available to give her whatever help she needs. So, we will have to wait and see what happens.

Sing His Praises have a few scheduled appearances. I'm not sure how it will all work out when school starts. The students will have their academic responsibilities to contend with as well as sports and other school activities. We will certainly miss Grace's contribution if she is forced to move. Also, I will have a full schedule limiting my availability. So, there again, we will have to see what we can work out. I'm sure we will, at least, be able to participate at some of the Sunday services.

I guess that about covers what is happening here.

I hope this finds you all well and enjoying the final weeks of summer.

I'll be seeing you soon

Love,
David

Saturday morning David picked Grace up promptly at 7:30 A.M. He wasn't sure how long it would take to get to the academy but thought it probably would be about two hours. He was glad she had accepted his offer to drive as it was apparent she was tense and having difficulty in controlling her anxiety. Given David's normal cheerful disposition, it wasn't long before Grace began to relax. They arrived in ample time with only a short wait before Grace was ushered into the interview room.

David had given her a big smile, a wink and a thumbs up reassuring her she had nothing to worry about! However, when he sat back down on the bench to wait, he was as nervous as a duck out of water. He tapped his feet on the floor, stared at the door she had entered, paced the floor—and prayed for God's blessing on the outcome.

At last! The door opened and he heard Grace say, "Thank you," as she shut the door behind her and entered the hallway. David could not tell by her expression what the outcome was. He knew though, if she had been accepted she would be smiling from ear to ear. This was not the case.

He walked over to her and said with concern, "How did it go? Was it very stressful?"

"No David, they were very nice and..." she smiled adding, "encouraging! I feel I have a chance that the grant will be approved. They will let me know within a few days."

David sighed with relief as he thought, *There's still hope for the grant...* However, he sympathetically looked at her and said, "You won't know for a few days!? I don't think I'll be able to survive that!"

She answered him in pretense sympathy, "I know it will be difficult but if you try hard enough I'm sure you will survive." She then continued in a teasing demanding tone, "However, right now **you** can take **me** out to lunch! I'm starving!"

"That's a great idea!" was David's quick reply.

They were on the drive home after their lunch when David glanced over at Grace and noticed she seemed relaxed and content. There was something that had been bothering his conscience and this seemed like a good time to approach it.

He sincerely said, "Grace, I know it was presumptuous of me to make an appointment for you without consulting you first.... I understand if it had annoyed and possibly angered you."

She quickly responded without hesitation, "Nothing could be further from the truth! I was shocked and thrilled that you had persevered to the point of giving me this opportunity......However, I must confess that I did not tell you some good news I had received that day as it conflicted a bit with yours."

"Really?!" David responded in surprise.

"I was offered the promotion to insurance underwriter and had to give my decision as of Friday, which was yesterday, if I wanted the position."

"You're kidding me! I can't believe this!... Grace, what a conflicting situation for you!...What answer did you give them?"

"It is amazing how we put ourselves through so much distress when the answer is obvious.

I simply told them the <u>truth</u>, that there was a good possibility of my resigning. They greatly appreciated my honesty and decided to wait until this coming Friday to fill the position, at which time I could give them my answer. I also explained today at the interview my situation and my appreciation if it was at all possible to notify me of their decision by Thursday."

David replied in a meditative manner, "You're right, Grace. As it says in Ephesians 4:25 'Therefore each of you must put off falsehood and speak truthfully'. The results you received substantiates the power of truth. Unfortunately, we fall short of obeying this more often than we realize as we frequently hedge around it.".....He paused a moment and then replied in an optimistic voice, "So, you are guaranteed of the promotion if the grant doesn't come through! That's great! You deserve it!"

"Thank you David, for all your support and enthusiasm." The tone of her voice reflected her deep feelings for the friend he had become.

They rode in silence for a short distance when Grace asked, "Where did you grow up? What was your childhood like?"

"I have a vague memory of living in a city apartment with my parents and older brother. We weren't there long when we moved into a house on the outskirts of Spring Valley. That's where I grew up. I have an older and younger brother plus my sister who is the youngest. We had a lot of good times together. After we moved there my father's work continued to take up more and more of his time. He had to travel into Lupton which was quite a distance making it a long day for him. He spent very little time with us kids as the years went by...... I missed the fun we used to have."

Grace noticed the melancholy tone of his voice and felt compassion for him. She asked with a bit of an upbeat sound to her voice in hopes of cheering him, "What did you do after you graduated high school?"

David laughed and responded, "Good question Grace! Actually, it really started in the beginning of my junior year. My dad was anything but a handy man around the house or property. So my mom always had to hire someone for any needed repairs.

There was in the village a retired elderly man who was always referred to as the Town's Handyman. One day he was repairing the pipe under the sink. I was keeping out of the way but still trying to see what he was doing. He asked me to please get him the wrench from his tool box, which I readily did. That was the beginning of my career!"

Grace laughed, "That was the beginning of your career? Now you're teasing me."

"No, that's the truth!" David replied emphatically. "He hired me on the spot to be his gopher. So, whenever I had free time I worked with him. Of course the pay was minimal. He was a very talented man who could do just about anything and was a master at it. He taught me plumbing, heating and electrical. He was planning on retiring in the near future. When I graduated I continued to work with him full time. My pay was increased since I now was more than a gopher. I was able to do many of the jobs myself. He retired within a year and I took over as the Town's Handyman. I studied up on woodworking, painting. roofing and even taking care of a dairy farm so the farmer could go on vacation. Within a year or so, I was truly the Town's Handyman and I couldn't have been any happier! Of course I didn't make a lot of money. The town and it's surrounding areas were just ordinary people managing to make ends meet. Then there was the older segment as well." David's voice now filled with exuberance as he continued, "They were the best customers! I would get home made cookies, cake and even pies! Along with that were wonderful interesting stories of the past events of their lives. Much better than money, a movie or reading a book." He sighed and along with the sigh Grace sensed he wished he was still the Town's Handyman!

She couldn't help herself as she asked, "David, what made you decide to attend college?"

"That's another story, but I will give you the short version. One day I decided I wanted to see and know more about peoples' lives. So I set out on a journey covering many areas of our country. I saw the affluent neighborhoods, but I also saw the complete opposite which outnumbered the affluent. I felt God's message, it was time for me to travel a different road than the one I was on. I knew I had to step forward, earn my degree and use it to help the oppressed and anyone else who crosses my road who is in some kind of need. I must admit children and young adults concern me the most. That' s it!"

"From what I've seen you certainly have already accomplished part of your goal even before attaining your degree. You have done so much with the teenagers. You relate to them so well which makes you an excellent teacher and role model."

"Do you honestly think teaching is my forte?"

"Yes, I do."

David remained quiet absorbing her answer.

*****

It was Tuesday morning and David had just finished cleaning up from his breakfast. The phone rang interrupting his thoughts. He picked the receiver up and waited for the other person to speak. This habit was due to the previous threats he had received.

A man's voice inquired, "Have I reached Mr. David Roberts?"

David decided the caller sounded legitimate and answered, "Yes."

"Mr. Roberts I represent the owner of the empty warehouse. You have called previously expressing an interest in this building. Are you still interested?"

David was shocked and excitedly answered, "Yes, I am."

"Fine, when is it convenient to come to a meeting?"

"I could come today at any time."

"Good. 10:30 this morning. The Business Enterprise Bldg. on 66 Main Street, Second Floor Office number 210. Looking forward to seeing you."

He hung up.

David arrived promptly for his 10:30 appointment with conflicting thoughts of the reasons and purpose causing such a drastic change from his previous calls. He entered the office and the man seated behind the desk, immediately stood up. He walked toward David with an outstretched hand and enthusiastically said, "I assume you are the miraculous Mr. David Roberts! I'm Mr. Ronald Green. I spoke with you on the phone."

Needless to say, David was stunned by the greeting. He reached forward shaking hands and replied, "I am David Roberts...." he then laughed slightly and said, "however as regards miraculous?—I greatly doubt that!"

He led David towards the inner office door commenting, "I realize you cannot possibly know what you have achieved!" He gave a light knock on the door as he opened it and announced, "Mr. Roberts, this is Mr. Sills who owns the warehouse."

The man stood up from behind his desk, also extending his hand and spoke softly, "I am pleased you were available to meet with me so promptly."

David went over and as he completed the handshake said, "I am so grateful for this opportunity to speak with you." He studied the man. There was something familiar about him but he couldn't place him.

"Please sit down, Mr. Roberts." He gestured to the chair in front of his desk as he sat back down. He glanced up at David and said, "Now, I understand you have plans for this building."

David hesitated, *how could he know I have* plans *for the building?* "You are right, I do. I must let you know up front that I do not have the funds to purchase it. However, I do have some other ideas which might interest you."

He looked directly at David and said, "Yes, I'm aware of that."

David was shocked! Those eyes! He recognized him! The Soup Kitchen! The man who most of the time kept his head down and hardly spoke. He recalled when he talked about the warehouse a mumbled voice inquired what he would do with it. The man before him now was clean shaven, dressed in an expensive suit and represented an efficient business man. It was hard to believe he was the same person David knew.

Mr. Sills smiled and replied, "So, you finally recognized me! I wasn't sure you would. I know you don't have the funds but I have a proposition for you. I plan to keep the warehouse and establish it as a charitable organization thus making it tax free. I will check with the church and allot them the space they need. No rent of course. They will have access to the use of the gym. I approve of all of your suggestions and I want you to periodically keep track that the renovations follow the plan. That is my proposition. What is your answer?"

When David recovered from the realization of Mr. Sills' offer he answered, "Do I understand you just want me to make sure the plans are followed? I really don't have the knowledge beyond that. Also, I'm a bit short of time due to attending college."

"I understand that. There is one other stipulation <u>you must agree to.</u> You are <u>not</u> to reveal to anyone, most importantly those who come to the soup kitchen and including the volunteers, <u>who I am.</u>

This is very important to me!"

"I agree to honor your request."

"Excellent!" Mr. Sills continued, "Once I get all the inspections and the required legal forms completed and approved I will get in touch with you and we can proceed on the renovations."

"That will be fine. I know the paper work can take some time."

"No doubt about that! On your way out stop at the desk as Mr. Green needs some further information from you. At that time tell him I said to fill you in on the details. He will understand what I mean by this statement. I look forward to working with you."

David went directly to Mr. Green's desk. Once they had completed the necessary paper work David said hesitantly, "Mr. Sills said that you are to fill me in on the details?"

Mr. Green sighed, "I expected he would want me to tell you. This is confidential and something yet to this day, he cannot verbalize himself. Nine years ago his wife and three children were killed in an airplane crash."

David gasped revealing his deep sympathy. After a moment, he commented, "That's why he became a vagrant?"

"Yes. He couldn't endure to remain in the house with all the memories. He lost all interest in living and I believe, at times, he considered taking his own life. He couldn't do that as it went against his religious beliefs. He took only the meagre necessities to survive on the street and made that his home these nine years. My theory is, he made this choice in the hope of getting sick and dying, thereby not exactly taking his own life. In spite of it all, he still is a kind, caring man. I deliver a considerable cash amount to the Soup Kitchen every two months."

David nodded, "Paul told me about that and it has him puzzled as to who the donator is."

He smiled, "I imagine it would be mind-boggling. A business envelope with the words printed on the front, 'Donation for the Soup Kitchen in the care of Paul, Supervisor' and just the cash inside the envelope. He looks at me in the hope I will give him a clue. Of course I can't do that so I just relay Paul's sincere 'Thanks'. It wouldn't surprise me if he goes back to living on the streets once this project gets underway...I really wish I could have heard your speech!... They must have been emotionally powerful moving words to have made Vincent decide to come back into the world with such enthusiasm to complete this project!... That's why I called you miraculous....No one has been able to get any kind of response from him the entire nine years!"

"Well, I'm sure it wasn't me. I believe God touched his heart and he responded."

"I like the way you think."

David smiled, "I'll be anxiously waiting for your call. Enjoy the rest of your day."

He left the building with a spring to his steps. He could hardly believe that the warehouse was going to be renovated. Since he was in the area of the police station, he decided to stop in and inquire regarding the last note that was left in his mailbox.

As soon as he entered the room the officer behind the desk greeted him, "Mr. Roberts, I was just about to call you with regards to the threatening note."

David walked up to the desk, "Well, that's why I'm here. I assume once again there weren't any helpful fingerprints or other signs to give an indication as to who the writer is or from any location."

"I'm sorry to say, but you are right. We have nothing to go on. Are you sure you don't have any inkling, no matter how foolish it might sound, as to who is harassing you? I must admit, it is a rather strange request they are making."

"I haven't got a clue. I guess we'll just have to wait and see what happens when the new semester starts. Thanks for trying. Have a good day."

He left the police station and headed for home.

*****

It was early Wednesday evening and David was relaxing in his comfortable chair, reading when he was interrupted by the phone. As he was walking over to answer it he wondered if it might be Grace. Much to his delight, he was correct.

"Hi David, this is Grace. I just received a call from the Academy." She continued in an excited voice, "I've been accepted! I got the grant!"

"Wow! That's terrific, Grace! I wonder, do you feel like taking a walk in the park and sitting on our favorite bench to watch the sunset. You can fill me on all the details."

"That sounds wonderful!"

"Great! I'll be there in about 35 minutes. That O.K.?"

"That's perfect."

David was lucky and found a parking space near Grace's building. He practically ran up the stairs in his excitement to see Grace and congratulate her.

One knock was about all he managed before the door flew open and a beaming Grace greeted him.

"I can't believe it David! Thank you so much!" She wanted to wrap her arms around him and give him a big hug, but she refrained from doing that.

He had a broad grin on his face and said with deep emotion, "Congratulations! I'm so happy for you!" He was also holding back the same feeling as Grace's. So, there they stood face to face in the joy of this blessing. After a brief second, David asked, "Are you ready? We don't want to miss the sunset!"

"Yes. Let's go!" was Grace's spontaneous reply.

It was a pleasant evening for their walk along the park's path to their favorite spot. There weren't many days left in the month of August before September and fall would be upon them. Grace was excitedly telling David some of the details regarding the grant. "I can't possibly commute from Eagerton to Morgan City and I know you are concerned and want to help me with the move. But, guess what?"

David grinning replied, "I don't know. What? Are you planning on setting up camp some place?

Be kinda cold during the winter months don't you think?"

She gently punched him in the arm and said, "Don't be a wise guy!"

David made a big show of rubbing his arm and said, "You don't have to get so rough. So tell me 'What' is What?"

She gave him a sidewise glance and answered. "What!" she said emphatically picking up on David's pun "happens to be an available room with bath and kitchenette included in the main building….and… which I can have just by working part time for them. There really isn't any specific time schedule. It's just being available when the need arrives. I believe it will be mostly clerical work during the busiest times of the semester. I probably will have to give up several Saturdays."

David replied still with a slight smirk, "That's a great 'What'."

She raised her eyebrows and answered, "Yes, it is a great 'What' and I forgot to tell you there is a bed, dresser and floor lamp. I will need to get a small desk and lamp for doing my assignments."

"Wow! That is one terrific 'What'."

Grace just looked at him and rolled her eyes while David broke into a hearty laugh.

They arrived at their special bench and sat down. Grace continued to tell David the remaining details, "The move will be very easy because I live in a furnished apartment. It probably will be just boxes."

David quickly interjected, "If it's O.K. with you I'd be more than happy to help. You just have to tell me when and what you need me to do."

"Oh, you can be sure I will do that!" she said sternly while smothering a smile.

David quickly turned his head looking at her with wide eyes, "Woe! What have I gotten myself into? A beautiful Simon Legree?"

"You never can tell," Grace said laughing and then added softly, "Thanks for the compliment."

"You're welcome," he replied quietly.

She continued, "I will notify the Insurance Company tomorrow morning when I arrive at work.

They may request me to stay on until the end of August. Then I would be able to train the person taking my place making a smoother transition. Staying the extra time would not hinder me at all."

"That would work out good as I was planning on going home for a few days. I would be back in time to help you."

They both settled back and gazed in awe at the breath-taking vision before them. David reached over slowly and gently took hold of Grace's hand and said softly, "You're going to make a terrific teacher!"

She glanced over at him and felt a short ache in her heart as she thought, *I'm going to miss you so much!*

They sat in silence each lost in the ever changing scene before them and their own thoughts......

which in a sense seemed to be drawing them emotionally closer.

*****

David was getting ready to pick Grace up and go to the Soup Kitchen to help with the Sunday dinner. He was deep in thought as he had some concerns regarding keeping the identity of Mr. Sills a secret, since some of the members had already made comments of missing him and were worried. He would need to avoid being involved in these conversations as much as possible. However, he was more disturbed about when they find out about the restoration and that all the suggestions he had verbalized to them recently were being done. Also, how could he keep it a secret that he was over-seeing the compliance of the plans? It would be obvious to them that he knew about it previously and did not tell them. He came to the conclusion he must tell them something now......but what?

Just as he was getting in the car, Rick drove in. David asked jokingly since their paths seem to cross infrequently, "Hey, Stranger! Good to see you!...Are you planning on coming to the Soup Kitchen?"

Rick replied apologetically, "I'm sorry but I have some other plans today. I'll miss being there. I always enjoy helping out. I'm planning on being there next Sunday."

"O.K. Have a good evening!" David continued getting into his car and headed out to get Grace.

It was another enjoyable late afternoon Sunday gathering at the Soup Kitchen. Once the blessing was said, the people enjoyed their meal along with conversation, music, singing and laughter.

When everyone had left, the volunteers proceeded with cleaning up. David decided to tell them the news he had.

"Can I have your attention for a minute? I have some terrific news to tell you." They quieted down eager to hear what he had to say.

"First of all and very important—I want to make this perfectly clear. I am obligated to confidentiality and can only tell you the facts that I give you now. I'd greatly appreciate your not asking me for any further information." He paused, took a deep breath and continued, "The warehouse is going to be renovated and established as a Charitable Service Building. The renovations will be based on the plans I had mentioned to you awhile ago."

This announcement was followed with clapping and loud shouts of joy.

Paul stepped up alongside of David putting his hands up to quiet down the group. He turned to David and said, "Obviously, God liked your plans."

David replied, "Well, I took your advice and got out of God's way and left it in His hands,"

Paul put an arm around David's shoulders and said, "When you did that, you did it in faith. You're a good man David. You are always thinking of others. I'm grateful for the day you walked into my life."

The group spontaneously reacted with a round of applause expressing total agreement. Now David humbly raised his hands up for them to stop. When all was quiet he said, "I don't know how long it will be before the renovations start. We all know of the red tape involved in any project of this kind. But what I think we should do now is—take a moment and offer our prayers of gratitude."

They responded immediately bowing their heads and each silently praying their own prayer of thanks for God's gifts of love.

They were considerate of David's request and did not approach him with questions. They returned to cleaning up, talking amongst themselves about this unexpected blessing.

*****

David was busy packing his duffle bag in preparation of leaving in the morning for his visit with his family. Grace had called informing him she would be working the extra week training her replacement. That had made it a good time for his trip.

He was standing in his bedroom contemplating if he had everything packed that he would need when the phone rang. He sighed and went into the living room where the phone was located. He hardly got the earpiece to his ear when the muffled voice said, "You're time has just about, reached the point of running out! Warnings are done, This is the final one!" Dial tone immediately followed.

David sighed and thought, *Good, no more messages. Maybe they have given up…or are making plans to injure me or worse. I am not going to let this person or persons cause me any more anxiety.*

He bowed his head and offered a prayer for God's protection and guidance adding a prayer for the person or persons who evidently were in need.

CHAPTER 16

September 1950

Dear Mom and Family,

It was great to be home! I'm glad we had plenty of time together, catching up on what's going on in our lives and the fun times shared! Of course I made sure I got my full share of Mom's cooking and baked goods! I'm pleased I was able to get around and visit some friends and reminisce of my days as the town's handyman and other fond memories. The saying, 'There's no place like home'
sure came from the heart.

Gertrude, the elderly lady I visit fre-quently, has invited me to her birthday party on Sept. 7ᵗʰ.

I will make it a point to stop in for a short visit but will try to avoid being there for the actual party.

I feel that's the time for her family and relatives.

Nothing else new since my visit.

Until next time....

Love,
David

David had just sat down at the table to eat his lunch when Rick came in the door. He was surprised to see Rick at this time of the day and asked, "What are you doing home? Did you take the day off?"

"No, I quit. I felt like having time off before the semester starts, so I quit my part-time job sooner than I had originally planned."

"Good for you! That was a smart decision."

Rick pulled out a chair and sat down at the table, "Yeah, it gives me some quality time during the day before going to my night time job. How are things with you especially now that Grace will be moving away?"

David slightly hesitated as he answered, "I'm fine…Of course I'm going to miss Grace just as a whole lot of other people will."

Rick, with a silly grin on his face, sat there staring at David.

"What's that look supposed to mean?" David asked.

Sarcastically Rick replied, "You're going to miss her just like every one else!" He shook his head and continued, "This is Rick you're talking to and I know you very well. You have feelings for her. She's not just another friend. The distance along with both of your schedules and other commitments is going to keep you apart. It's going to be difficult for both of you and it's going to be for a good length of time before you get your degrees."

David conceded, "You're right. It is going to be difficult. Believe me, if she feels the same as I do, we will see each other frequently. There's always Sundays, holidays, along with semester breaks. I can make the trip there and back in one day if necessary."

Rick was quiet for a moment, then nodded his head and said, "That's true."

David knew that Rick had other thoughts, but evidently did not want to verbalize them. He was pretty sure he knew what was troubling him, so he decided to let him know he was aware of the other conflicts he would face. "Rick, I know I will have some hard choices to make. The Soup Kitchen

Sunday night dinners along with other meals, the Sing His Praises, and helping other students with homework problems. It will all work out. I know in some way God will guide me. He will help me find others to fill in who will find the joy of serving God as well as realizing they have talents and abilities they weren't aware of. Actually, it will definitely be a blessing!"

"Well, you've got a volunteer here whenever I'm not in class or working. You can count on me! However, I don't think I'll be much help with Sing His Praises. Carrying the hymnal is the only way I can carry a tune."

"I'll remember that." David smiled and then paused a moment continuing with deep emotion, "Thanks, Rick! You're a true friend! I'm grateful for the person who pushed me on the stairs that first day…. I might not have met you otherwise."

Rick became very serious as he stood up and said emphatically, "God certainly blessed me by putting me there….He does work in strange ways… doesn't He?" Rick then headed over to the kitchen cabinet, opened the door and began searching for something.

David called over to him and said, "We ate up all of my Mom's cookies that I brought from my visit."

Rick turned and looked at him very despondent and asked, "When are you going to visit again?

How about next week?"

"Dream on Rick, dream on! Probably not 'til Thanksgiving."

Rick sighed and took out a box of store bought cookies. As he passed David going towards his room, he mumbled, "Life sure is tough!"

David laughed and said, "You'll survive!"

"How can you be so sure?" Rick retaliated as he went into his room to his desk.

*****

David turned into Gertrude's driveway and noticed another car parked there. He figured it was probably some of the family preparing for the party. He didn't want to be in the way so he would cut his visit short. He picked up his present for Gertrude. It consisted of a book of crossword puzzles and a box of assorted butter cookies from the bakery. Both items were favorites of hers. He had wrapped them in flowery birthday paper as well as topping it off with a special birthday card. He walked cheerfully up the front steps and rang the bell.

The door opened and a young woman stood facing him. To his alarm he was greeted with an accusing, "You!" He sensed her emotions went from, shock to fear and then to hate! He glanced over his shoulder thinking someone else had arrived that he wasn't aware of. No one was there! Looking back at the woman there was no doubt that she had all she could do to stop herself from physically attacking him with the intention, as the proverbial saying goes, to scratch his eyes out!

There was something slightly familiar about her. All of a sudden he remembered. *She works in the college's office. I never spoke to her but she saw me and heard my name as I spoke with the other secretary. She had access to my file thereby knowing my address and phone number. Could it be? Is she my nemesis.? The driving me off the road, the notes and phone calls all came late in the evening or at night. She had access to my car parked at the college as well as being aware of my schedule. The only catch is—who was the man that shoved me on the stairs? More specifically—Why Does She Hate Me!?*

Just then, Chad came to the door and started to ask, "Who is…" He stopped short noticing his sister, Trudy's emotional state. He quickly eased her onto the porch, stepped out himself and quietly shut the door behind them.

He turned to his sister and asked? "What's wrong?"

She quickly replied with malice as she stared at David, "There will never be another Robert's lawyer to set murderers free, if I can do anything about it!"

David was confused. He really did not know what she was referring to, other than the fact she evidently meant his father. He calmly replied, "My degree will be in family law. I have no idea what you are referring to. I assume because of my father you have been the one who tampered with my car, drove me off the road and sent warning notes along with threatening phone calls? Did you arrange the shove on the stairs as well, or was that truly an accident?"

Chad now showed worried anxiety as he looked at his sister and asked, "What is he talking about? Did you really do those things?"

She ignored her brother and looked at David still with hate and tears in her eyes and said, "You're father set a driver, who was wild, reckless and an uncaring thrill seeker free who killed my younger brother. When the trial was held he also managed to make it look like my brother was at fault and once again this man was acquitted...... I wonder how many more people he injured or killed?"

The tears rolled down her cheeks and her brother wrapped his arms around her, holding back his own tears. He looked over appealing to David, "Please don't bring charges against her."

However, David as he was listening to Trudy's explanation had recalled that terrible hate which had surged through his body as regards to Milano who was making plans that could kill or injure innocent people. He had felt that horrible hate towards Milano and it was because of people he didn't know...... He looked at Trudy and her brother now who were grieving at the unnecessary loss of a loved one—their younger brother—Yes, that certainly could cause an uncontrollable anger which turned into uncontrollable hate.

The thought of bringing charges against Trudy had never entered his mind. There was one requirement he was going to try to insist on.

When Trudy and Chad had regained control David said, "I have no intentions of bringing charges against Trudy but I do have one request I am asking for."

He directed his request to Trudy, "I would like you to make an appointment with the minister of the

Christian Fellowship Church of Eagerton. I sincerely believe he can be of help to you and more than likely guide you to other sources of support."

He looked at Chad and said, "She needs some professional help to deal with this grief and hate that she has bottled up inside her for many years. Can I count on you to see that she has at least one meeting with him?"

"Of course you can! I might schedule a meeting for myself as well."

Now that Trudy had met David face to face the hostility towards him started to fade as the memories came back to how he had helped her grandmother, a total stranger. She also realized her grandmother had seemed happier since his visits along with the thoughtful gifts he gave her from time to time. She saw him at this moment for the man he was.—Kind, Caring, and Forgiving.- A strong guilt feeling over-took her for what she had done. She stepped forward facing him and said in a broken voice, "I am so sorry!"

He looked at her with compassion and said, "I have forgiven you... Now, all I ask is….that you forgive yourself!"

"I just would like to clear up one item that really is nagging at me—The man that pushed me on the stairs—was that a true accident?"

"I'm sorry to say it wasn't. It's easy to find bullies on campus who will do anything for a few dollars! Let me help to clarify some other details you might be wondering about. I hired a private investigator for one week to follow you. That is how I knew about the Soup Kitchen, the church you attend, your favorite diner and wherever else you went that week. However, you did not go to my grandmother's. Unfortunately, my brother and grandmother could not remember your name. There was a good reason since both were under the stress of Grandma's fall and it was a brief encounter." She now added with a slight tease in her voice, "And…of course, my grandmother didn't really care since she has her own special name for you."

David slightly blushed feeling a bit self-conscious because of their pretenses—but Gertrude enjoyed it so much and he had to admit it was a lot of fun. He had to also acknowledge he really would have preferred it to have remained just between the two of them.

At that moment the front door opened and another young lady stepped out onto the porch and said slightly scolding, "Why haven't you come in? Grandma's wondering who was at the door and is now becoming concerned since it was getting to be quite awhile."

Chad quickly spoke up, "I'm sorry Sophie. We were just about to go in. First though, I want you to meet David, Grandma's good friend."

He turned to David and said, "This is my wife, Sophie."

David extended his hand and cordially said, "Nice to meet you."

A large smile overtook her face as she responded to David's greeting, "It is such a pleasure to meet Grandma's Prin…." she quickly stopped herself and said, "good friend!"

David smiled at her near error and then went on to say, "I think we should go in now as I am anxious—" he paused and with mischievous eyes accompanied with a big grin completed his sentence, "to wish 'My Lady' a happy birthday!"

They all chuckled as they entered the house.

David had decided they all knew about the pet names for each other so why not have fun with it.

As they entered the house, Chad told David to go ahead and visit with his grandmother while they continued to get things ready for the party.

"Thanks, I won't stay too long," David replied as he didn't want to be in the way of their finishing the preparations.

"Stay as long as you like! Actually, I was hoping you would stay for the party," Chad exclaimed.

Just then Gertrude called out, "Did I just hear my prince?"

David smiled and shook his head, "I do believe I am being summoned. I wish I could stay, but I have some things that need to be taken care of. Thanks for the invite."

He turned and entered the living room commenting softly, "Yes, it is I."

"What took you so long to come in?"

"I was getting to know your family. They are very special people just like their grandmother."

"Flattery will get you no-where. Only because it is the right thing to do, I will forgive you."

"That is very kind of you," he said as he sat down in a chair next to her's and handed her his present."

She was thrilled with both items and thanked him for always noticing her favorite things!

There would be no Scrabble game during this visit since there wasn't a table to set it up on due to the party preparations. David suggested the idea of doing a crossword puzzle together. They would keep score to see who gave the most correct answers. Needless to say, David suggested some weird words or made-up words when he didn't know the answer. They laughed a lot and teased each other as they completed the puzzle. It was a close game but Gertrude won and, of course, lauded it over David.

She noticed David glimpse at his watch and knew it was nearing time for him to leave. A little sigh slipped out as she took a wishful glance at the record player.

David got up from his chair and said, "You didn't think I would leave without our dance, did you?"

He went over and put a record on. He returned to Gertrude, bowed, extended his hand, and invited her to dance with him.

She smiled up at him, put her hand in his and stood.

The grandchildren heard the music and quietly went to the living room entrance. They stood in amazement as they watched their grandmother dancing with 'her prince'.

Chad astoundingly whispered, "I never thought about her dancing!"

Sophie commented, "She is so graceful and she looks so happy!"

Trudy added, "Her partner appears to be a professional! He certainly knows how to guide and move about the floor…A prince, indeed!"

Chad quietly said to Sophie, "I see where I need to improve my dancing. I don't want to step on Grandma's toes on my visits with her."

She replied, "How come you never worried about my toes?"

He looked at her and said, "Your toes are young. Grandma's are old!"

She gave him a look of disbelief.

They watched a few minutes longer then returned to the few things left to finish the party preparations.

After completing their final dance, David escorted Gertrude to her chair. He told her that on his next visit she should be prepared as he was going to win the Scrabble games.

She replied, "Perhaps… Miracles can happen."

He laughed and gave her a quick hug and whispered another Happy Birthday wish.

Before he left he said goodbye to the grandchildren and expressed his appreciation for their invite to stay for the party and for their full approval of his visits to their grandmother.

Walking towards his car an idea came to him. He could drive to Lupton where his father's law practice had been and visit the newspaper office. He would request to search the archives to find if there was an article on the accident that Trudy mentioned. He figured he had a ball-park idea of the possible few years to search. His other errands could wait. He drove to Lupton and quickly located the building. Fortunately, an elderly man was still employed who had memories of his father. He accompanied him to the archives and was able to narrow down the search as well as helping to look for the specific article. After searching awhile David pulled up an issue and there on the front page it glared at him, causing his blood to run cold.

Would-Be Killer Set Free

Mayor's son goes free for the second time.

Adam Roberts, his lawyer, finds another technicality to have charges of reckless driving dropped. Story on Pg.3

David reluctantly turned to the page and read the article. It was rather brief but it was apparent that substantial evidence was not presented to confirm the son had been driving recklessly. The case lacked a reliable witness to the incident. The charges were vague and were dismissed.

David continued to search further not eager to find another article, but knew within his heart he would. Two months' issues later, there it was:

Mayor's Son Kills Pedestrian

loses control due to speeding. Story on Page 2.

Once again he reluctantly turned to the page and read the article.

The accident happened at late dusk. The driver insisted the boy had stepped out in front of the car just as he was approaching, making it impossible to avoid hitting him. The lawyer for the plaintiff argued the driver was recklessly driving at a high speed, losing control of the car causing him to hit the boy. There were no witnesses to the accident.

David's father had the power of mesmerizing his listeners and thereby succeeded to influence the jury to the point of complete agreement to his concept of the incident. This resulted in his winning the case, setting the driver free again.

*****

David had many mixed emotions when he left the newspaper's office. He felt the need to speak with the family's lawyer and good friend. He drove to his office which was located in Lupton.

He was pleasantly surprised when Tom was available to see him. Once the initial greetings were done they settled down in Tom's office in preparation for the business at hand.

"So… David! What brings you here? How can I help you?"

"The best way you could help me would be to tell me—my father wasn't bought off by influential elected officials when they or their family members were guilty of crimes!"

Tom exclaimed, "Wow! I wasn't expecting that question!"

"So…what's the answer, Yes or No?"

"I cannot in all honesty say that I know for a fact that statement is true! There appeared to be instances where that might have been the case." He paused, obviously trying to organize his thoughts.

"Your father was an outstanding lawyer! It was early in his career when he became known for his expertise. A prestigious law firm offered him a position and he accepted. He had to take the cases they gave him. He always gave his clients the best he could! He thrived on challenges and on winning! Unfortunately, he got caught up in the affluent lifestyle and the financial gains and paid little attention to the on-going results of some of his cases. He was paid very well for every case he was assigned. I do not know if he received any added amount for defending elected officials or any others. In other words using your description—bought off... For what it's worth, my gut feeling is: he did not."

David asked, "Do you know of the case that entailed setting a reckless driver free several times and the final result was that he killed a young boy and was once again exonerated?" He added angrily, "Thanks to my father!"

"Yes, I do. That occurred in his later years and had quite an affect on him. It caused him to regret that first weakness of compromise when he strayed from his initial desire to become a lawyer so he could be an advocate for the low income sector."

They both were quiet for a moment. David had just currently became aware of the reason behind his father's choice of his profession. He grew up in the knowledge that his father was an exceptional lawyer but completely unaware of his cases. He lived in the small town of Spring Valley miles away from the city of Lupton and never had access to the city's newspaper. As an adult he was happy with what he was doing and had no desire to go to college until now.

David broke the silence, "I imagine I still have a substantial amount of funds left from Dad's inheritance. I don't have a good feeling about that money due to these recent facts. I think I will get a job and work my way through college as my brother Adam did…. Do what you want with <u>that </u>money. I have no use for it!"

David was about to stand up when Tom quickly said, "Please David, wait a moment! You're making a decision due to hurt and anger. Just give me ten minutes more."

David settled down again in his chair and said, "O.K. Tom because you are a special friend, I'm interested in what you have to say."

"First of all neither of us know if any of that money is corrupt which happens to be the premise you are assuming. However, what difference does it make since it's providing you the advantage to get your degree which will be helping and caring about other people? Doesn't God take bad and make it good?

You already have used some of it recently to help a family in need. Plus in the past you have done the same thing many times.

Since I'm the one who keeps track of your funds, I'm aware of what you do. What gain is there in your taking away your limited free time by working? Think, David, what do you do with that time? My interpretation is: Serving God.—. Soup Kitchen, Sing His Praises—and other activities of helping and cheering people up. I care about you and your family and I keep close track on how you all are. I deeply feel that God provided this money as part of his plans for you!......I guess my ten minutes are up."

David had sat quietly absorbing Tom's words. David's final thought was, *He's right...especially with Grace's moving away...I'd have no time for those services...he's also right, I made the decision feeling overcome by hurt and anger.* Once he acknowledged these facts, he felt a calm feeling travel through his body.

He answered Tom, "Thank you. You made a lot of sense and I agree with you. I won't get a job, I do have better things to do with that time." David stood up and shook Tom's hand finalizing their conversation.

Now Tom seemed to be showing a little anxiety as if he was holding back on something as he apprehensively said, "By the way David do you remember I suggested you should invest part of your inheritance since you weren't planning on college and you said, 'No. don't bother with anything like that.' Well, I took it upon myself to invest half of the money, knowing I had it covered should it fail.

It didn't fail so you have a good sum of money. I know that wasn't the right thing to do but it seemed like the wise thing to do."

"You did what!" David exclaimed. "No, it wasn't the right thing to do!...... However, I agree it was the wise thing to do! Thanks!"

They both had a good laugh as David left the office relieved of the uncomfortable mixed emotions he had come in with.

*****

It was late by the time David got back home. He was glad he had stopped for something to eat along the way. He felt exhausted. It had been quite an emotional day! He stretched out on the couch to relax. In his mind he went over the day's activities. He decided he would not contact the police to inform them he knew who was responsible for harassing him. They probably would want the name and details and he wasn't sure if they may feel it necessary to investigate further. Should they call him and inquire he could just say, 'The threats have stopped' and that should end the conversation and the entire episode.

He remembered he wanted to call Adam, his older brother, to make arrangements to meet with him. He needed to discuss an important matter with him as soon as possible. He got up and picked up the phone, hoping Adam would be available. He was successful in making the call and arranged a meeting for the next evening at 8:00 P.M. It was at a diner located approximately halfway between both of them.

*****

The next day he spent taking care of several details as well as helping Grace in her preparations for the move, which, now was only a few days away.

When evening came he left in ample time to be at the diner for his meeting with Adam. He arrived a few minutes prior to Adam's pulling into the parking lot. The two brothers greeted each other and then proceeded to enter the diner. They found a booth whose location appeared to provide a little more privacy.

Once their order was taken Adam asked, "Now, how can I be of help?"

"I've got an important decision to make and I would like to know what your advice would be with regards to it."

Adam was a bit hesitant since he didn't know what kind of advice David was looking for but he replied, "O.K."

"You probably remember when I told Mom and you I had decided to get a degree in law. I indicated to Mom that I would not stray from the goal I had made. Well, the situation is this:

I'm not sure I want to be a lawyer."

Adam was tempted to reply. But did not. He sensed David had more to tell him prior to his giving any comments or advice.

David continued to say, "Grace has constantly made comments about what a terrific teacher I would make for teenagers. She thinks that's the degree I'm aiming for. I have tried to tell her the truth many times, but I was always interrupted. Anyway, I really enjoy working with that age group. It's an exhilarating feeling when you see them grasp the solution of the problem they are having difficulty with. Also, they are complex and challenging and I learn from them as well as they from me.

"Now, it's a good thing you are sitting, because what I'm about to say next will probably shock you. My pastor insists that I would make an excellent minister! He has offered to assist me to get accepted into a seminary. I have gone with him many times on home visits and assisted in other ways as well. I can't find the exact words as to how these experiences affected me. I know it gave me the sensation of being helpful.

I feel like I'm in a traffic circle with these three roads each pulling me in their direction as I keep circling around. There isn't one that seems to have a greater pull than the others. I don't know which is the right road God wants me to take!"

He paused and looked at Adam and said, "You know me well. What do you think?"

Adam did not reply immediately. He was completely taken off-guard. Yes, he did know David well. He always sensed David kept hidden that serious, sensitive part of his being. In spite of that his usual up-lifting, joyous mannerism was also an integral part of him. He took delight in making people smile and laugh.

After a few moments, Adam answered, "David, you know I cannot tell you which of those roads you are to choose. That decision is yours only! I will, however, offer a suggestion that might help.

Think of each profession separately and seriously imagine what your life would be like as you fulfilled the demands of that profession. I'm not talking about making lists of pros and cons. I'm talking about searching your inner feelings regarding the aspects of the profession. Does the thought of the continuous days' requirements cause you any feelings of apprehension and to what degree?

Now, the most important question you must answer for each one after completing your imaginary life is—Do you have the sensation of contentment? God wants us to be happy! If it doesn't create that feeling – then it probably isn't the right choice.

I have one more comment that might inadvertently be causing some of your dilemma.

Do not be concerned with regards to Mom and your comment to her about not straying from the goal you have chosen. She understands we can feel deeply about something in the moment, but life gives us changes which affects our decisions and feelings.

One of Mom's desires for her children is that they find happiness. Keep that in mind. I'm afraid that's the best I have to offer."

"Your suggestion makes a lot of sense and I'm positive it will help. Now, I'm sure you have a choice of which one you think is best for me.—So, how about telling me? It might be of some help hearing your thoughts."

Adam laughed and replied, "Nice try David! Like I told you previously, that decision is entirely up to you! Yes, I do have a feeling for the choice I think is best…but I'm not telling you. I will not influence your decision! I will say this: that whichever road you choose will be serving God and I'm sure will please Him……. Just remember after analyzing the demands that each profession will require of you, make sure there is sufficient free time for all the other activities you enjoy. I'll be praying for God's guidance and will be anxious to know your decision."

"I'll call you when I decide." David then added sincerely, "I really felt the need to talk with you… Thank you for your support and for making the time to come. I know it's difficult for you due to your dedication to your patients to be available if a need occurs."

"Yes, I do have a dedication to my patients. I also have a dedication to my family as the Bible instructs us in 1 Timothy 5:8 that we are to be there for our immediate family, and to fail to do so, denies the faith and is worse than a disbeliever... David I'm always here for you. Never hesitate to call on me! Should there be a conflict, God will take care of the other need."

*****

David had set his alarm and was up before sunrise the next morning. He knew he had to make his decision quickly in order to arrange his college courses for the up-coming semester – especially if he decided to change his profession. He desired to be some place completely alone and surrounded by God's comforting presence as he analyzed his choices. He got in his car and drove to the park. He walked leisurely along the path letting the peace and quiet envelop him. He found a bench, sat down and looked at the sun now beginning to peak over the horizon. No one else appeared to be up and about, except David.

He said a prayer for help and guidance and then began analyzing following Adam's suggestion.

First-Lawyer:I haven't had any life experience in this profession, but I am knowledgeable as to what it does entail. I can imagine what a day would be like. He sat immersed losing himself in what that future would be like. Then he asked himself the two main questions as Adam had suggested.—*Degree of apprehension? Free time for the other things I really enjoy?*

Next-Teacher: I've had a touch of life experience here as I have spent time with teenagers, both tutoring and recreational. Of course, there's a lot more to teaching than that! He went through the same process as he did with the lawyer, culminating with the same two questions.

Minister: He sighed- *Why am I considering this? Do I really have the qualities for the ministry?* Remembering his minister's confidence in him had caused him to recall the times spent as they served people. So he decided he would put it to the test just as he had the others.

With closed eyes and in humble meditation he recalled each of the professions and compared the final results remembering Adam's emphasis of the words, 'apprehension and free time.'

He opened his eyes and gazed at the beautiful sunrise before him and felt a wonderful and exhilarating feeling overwhelm him!—He knew within his soul—the road God wanted him to pursue!

CHAPTER 17

September 1950 Continued

Dear Mom,

Just wanted to drop you a line to let you know I'm planning on a short visit. I don't know the exact day and there is the chance I might arrive before this letter. I realized there's no reason to always wait until I have several days before visiting. I can make the trip easily in one day. I wish I had thought about that sooner.

I'm looking forward to sitting with you at the kitchen table, having a cup of coffee (and hopefully some left over homemade

cookies) as we share our thoughts and memories. Just like we use to do!
>   *Look for me on your doorstep! Love,*
>>   *David*

As soon as David returned from the park, he had quickly written his letter and hurried downstairs to the mailbox for that day's pick-up. He wasn't confident that the letter would arrive before he did, but it was worth a try.

Returning to his apartment he went directly to the phone to call Adam as promised. He glanced at his watch and hoped it would be an appropriate time to call.

Adam answered within two rings.

David teasingly said, "What is this! You have to answer your phone? I thought you had a receptionist for that!" Then David added with a little sarcasm, "That's what the majority of doctors have -in case you don't know!"

Adam laughed and replied, "Well, I do—I still regress to the times when I didn't. Anyway, I was free and closest to the phone...I'm guessing this call is an answer I've been anxiously waiting for? I'll be honest, it's a little sooner than I expected. It was definitely a difficult decision to make!"

"Well, I'm really on a tight time schedule. So—do you want to guess? Or do you want me to just tell you?"

"Stop keeping me hanging, and tell me!"

"O.K. You ready?"

David heard a big sigh and had to stifle his urge to laugh and then replied, "I don't know, it might surprise you."

Now David heard an exasperated, muffled, "David!"

David became serious and answered, "I decided to become a minister!"

Adam's reaction was spontaneous, "Terrific! That's the best choice you could've made!"

David was caught off-guard—He did not expect that response.

He was brought out of his stupor by Adam's laughing reply, "I gather my reaction surprised you. Well, dear brother, that was my choice for you! I agree you would have made an excellent teacher and probably would have been mildly happy. But a lawyer?—no doubt successful in your goals—but miserable otherwise! These are my final evaluations."

David asked, "That was your choice when we were in the diner and you refused to tell me?"

"Yes. I did a little analyzing as we talked. Gave it a lot more thought after, as well as prayer."

"Please don't say anything to Mom or anyone else about the change. I plan to make a visit soon. I want to tell Mom myself in person. That's very important to me! Also, I don't want anyone else knowing before her, other than you."

"I fully understand and will honor your request. Thanks for taking me into your confidence.

Remember—I'm always here for you!" Then he added jesting, "That's what big brother's are for."

David jokingly responded, "Yeah! Along with giving orders to younger brothers reminding them your older and in charge!"

Defensively, Adam replied, "I never did that!"

David replied sarcastically, "No, of course not!"

Now they both broke out into laughter!

After gaining composure Adam said, "Love ya!"

David replied, "Same here," and hung up—ending the call.

Now he made the next important call and succeeded in getting an appointment to meet with his minister for early afternoon.

The morning was slipping by and he decided to call Grace and see if she would like to go to lunch with him. She was no longer working since her employment with the insurance company ended the last day of August. He wanted to spend as much time with her as possible before she left Eagerton.

She had the same feelings with regards to him. So, of course, she happily accepted his invitation.

During lunch they discussed the upcoming events for the next few days. That evening they had a practice rehearsal with Sing His Praises in preparation for the following evening's performance. Grace said her aunt and two cousins had made plans to spend the day after that with her, before she moved.

David decided that was a perfect day to visit his mother as he would be able to spend most of the day with her. This would depend, of course, on all things falling into place with his change of profession. He decided not to mention this as yet to Grace until after he met with his minister. He wasn't sure how involved the procedure might get. Of course the remaining free time of these two days would probably be spent at the Soup Kitchen. He always enjoyed spending more time with them during his vacations. He knew Grace would join him if she was available as she enjoyed it as much as he did.

After lunch, Grace had some chores to tend to and David went to his meeting with the minister.

The minister was seated on the patio by the flower garden area and called out to David as he was heading toward the church doors. "David! Over here! I felt this would be the perfect place to talk. I know how much you enjoy God's gifts of beauty."

"The fall flowers really are beautiful!" David replied as he went over and accepted the out-stretched hand of his exuberant minister! He commented as he sat down in his chair, "This is great!" He paused and added, "Well, I would say it is apparent you approve of my decision to go into the ministry."

This was followed by an ecstatic reply. "I most certainly do!"

They talked a little while on the demands, responsibilities, requirements and duties of the ministry.

Finally, the minister said, "I have already been in touch with the Divinity Seminary. You need to go to the office as soon as possible with the record of your completed college courses. They do offer some academic courses along with the theological requirements. You do not need an appointment. They are located a short distance north outside of Eagerton." The minister now handed a map to David.

He continued, "If you have already met all the required academic courses, you will be able to start this coming semester with the theological requirements."

"That would be great! I will head over there right away!" David stood up and gave the minister a hearty hand shake and an emotional, "ThankYou! Thank You so Much! I'll make sure you don't regret sponsoring me!"

The minister replied in complete confidence, "I have no concerns there!"

David went to his current college and requested the necessary records he needed as well as informing them that he may not be taking any further classes there. He explained that it would depend on whether he has met the required subjects at the seminary prior to starting the theological courses. They supplied him with what he requested and wished him good luck.

He had no difficulty in locating the building and the registration office. They recognized his name as soon as he introduced himself. They gave him forms to complete and he gave them the information he had brought. All things went along smoothly and to his delight he had met the requirements and would start immediately on the theological courses. They gave him his schedule and classes would begin in five days.

Before returning home, he stopped at the college again to inform them that he would not be taking any further courses. He thanked them for the good service and for the excellent professors he had encountered during his time there.

He returned home just in time to get a bite to eat and then get ready to pick Grace up for the rehearsal of Sing His Praises. Just as he was about to go out the door his phone rang. He rushed over and picked it up, "David speaking."

"This is Lester Reardon from the tenament. The bank has set an appointment for tomorrow morning at 10:00 A.M. Is that time OK for you? It appears things are in order and will just need our signatures. Of course if you have any other concerns you can bring them up prior to signing. Does this work out for you?"

"Yes, that's fine! I'm glad it has moved as quickly as it has. I'll see you there at 10:00 A.M. tomorrow!"

He got to Grace's on time and the rehearsal was excellent except for an underlying feeling of melancholy. The young people knew that this rehearsal and tomorrow's performance would be the last one with Grace for awhile. They all loved and respected her as well as enjoying her singing when she sang her solos.

*****

The next morning David met Grace for breakfast during which time he told her he was changing his choice of profession.

She asked with a slight disappointment in her voice which she was unable to conceal, "Then you're not going to be a teacher?"

David hesitated a moment, sighed a bit, and said, "Grace, I wasn't planning on teaching. Every time I went to tell you, I was interrupted, then I forgot about it. I was planning to be a lawyer but I know now that is not what I want to do. I did consider teaching. My decision, however, is the ministry. I'm sure this surprises you."

"The ministry!" She sat silently for a moment gazing at him recalling the things that had excited and motivated him and finally said, "That is the perfect choice for you!"

"You really think so?"

"Yes! I do! I admit I hadn't thought of it since I was so engrossed in thinking of you as a teacher. Do you know where the seminary is that you will be attending?"

"I'm already registered at the Divinity Seminary just north outside of Eagerton. My minister recommended me and everything fell into place. I start this coming semester."

"I couldn't be any happier for you! God has certainly cleared the road He wishes each of us to travel."

"No doubt about that! He has definitely blessed us!"

Before David knew it, it was time to leave for his morning meeting at the bank.

Mr, Reardon was already there and was excited and pleased to see David. "I can't thank you enough for what you are doing for me," he quickly said as David approached.

"My pleasure. I'm glad I'm able to help."

They entered the building and without having to wait, met with the bank representative.

Once seated in his office he stated, "I'm glad this was able to come to fruition since there were so many underlying legal complications." He handed each of them their copy of the contract for their approval or questions.

They both read it slowly and carefully and then looked at each other and nodded in agreement.

The representative handed them a pen.

Mr. Reardon signed first and then David co-signed and handed the documents back. The representative signed them plus one more transcript which now required Reardon's and David's signatures.

Once this was accomplished, all had their own copy of the legal document.

The representative said emphatically, "Well, Mr. Reardon! How does it feel to own three more apartment buildings?"

"A bit scary, but wonderful! Thanks to David for backing me up and making it possible."

"I wish you the very best! There would have been a lot of people homeless, if you hadn't taken over these tenements. They're in need of a lot of maintenance and repairs as Milano did very little in keeping them in good order. If you have any other needs don't hesitate to call on me."

*****

That evening's performance of Sing His Praises once again was received with an overwhelming applause stimulated by the emotional affect upon the audience. There were moments in between the selections when the chorus had difficulty in controlling their tears. This was due to the fact of Grace's leaving. She assured them that she would return whenever she could and join with them in a practice session or performance. This helped to ease the gloomy feeling.

*****

The next day and evening Grace spent with her aunt and cousins. They had an enjoyable time together reminiscing as well as creating new memories for the future years.

David left in the morning for his visit with his mother. She was expecting him since his letter had arrived prior. She had purposely baked cookies for their time together as well as a sufficient amount for him to take home.

He had his wish as they did sit at the kitchen table with coffee and cookies as they talked. He told her of his decision to become a minister. She was quite surprised as she had never thought of that profession for him. She couldn't be more pleased and she made this apparent to David. He felt relieved of that nagging concern of disappointing her.

They recalled some of his past antics of his childhood and youth which caused a great deal of laughter. He told her in more detail about Sing His Praises and the Soup Kitchen. She listened to him intently and observed him. It warmed her heart as she came to the conclusion that David had come to reconciling the underlying hurt his father had caused him—by ignoring David's desire to please him and become a lawyer.

They took a walk about the property enjoying the flower and vegetable gardens. They played some card and board games.

They ended their time together by playing the piano and singing hymns and their favorite songs.

This had been a day that fell in the category of cherished memories!

David got home in time to go to the Soup Kitchen for the evening meal. He had just placed a refill of vegetables on the serving table when he heard Don say. "Hey. Look who just came in!"

David startled, turned around and looked. Sure enough, there he was, Vincent Sills, owner of the warehouse. He walked bent over with his head down and got on the serving line. He reached Don holding his plate out for his portion of food.

Don said as he served him, "Welcome back! We missed you!"

Vincent just nodded his head and moved on.

Don commented, "He must have had his beard trimmed along with his hair. Hope he wasn't sick."

Paul had just come from the kitchen and saw the episode. He turned to David who was about to re-enter the kitchen and said softly, "How about that? Is that the same man who a few months ago had the habit of criticizing and judging people? That welcome was deep and sincere. I'm going to let him know that was a really nice thing he did," and he headed over toward Don.

Everyone had their food and David was going about visiting with the people. Vincent grabbed David's sleeve as he walked by him.

David nonchalantly bent over and Vincent whispered, "That man serving sounded as if he really meant what he said."

David whispered back, "He did! The people here were concerned about you." He quickly stood and walked away. He went over to the piano and asked for any requests. He received several and responded to them. He always sang some hymns ending the music. He then went into the kitchen to help.

Paul walked over to him and said, "You know I've been observing Don tonight and I came to the realization that he has changed a lot. He hasn't been critical or derogatory and he seems happier."

David replied, "Yes, I've been noticing it also. I think that through our prayer before our meals, along with Sunday's short service and the hymns and music, God has touched the critical part of his heart."

They stood for a moment in the kitchen and listened to the talking and laughter coming from the dining area.

Paul walked over to the door and gazed at the group of people enjoying their meal as well as each other. A few of the volunteers had also joined in. Paul turned to David and said, "I recall that first day you came and helped. You took time to visit with the people making them laugh and interact with each other. You opened my eyes to the realization of a service we were lacking,-the appreciation of each other...Then came Valentines' Day. And once again you reminded us of God's unfailing love.

This was our stepping stone to remember to offer our thanks and praise, drawing us closer to Him and each other!"

Just then Don came over to Paul with a broad smile and excitedly said, "Look! Our friend has raised his head and is slightly smiling! Isn't that great!?"

David silently sent a devout 'Thank You!'— God had healed part of Vincent's broken heart!

*****

Grace and David only had three days left before Grace would be leaving Eagerton. They both wanted to spend these days together. They succeeded in fulfilling their plans. They spent one day taking advantage of the available hiking trails in the area. Their second day they made a picnic lunch and went fishing. The third day they spent driving around the surrounding country roads and stopping to take in the spectacular scenery along the way. Of course, every evening they would take their walk in the park to their favorite bench and watch the sunset, staying until it became a bit difficult to see.

This was their last night as Grace had to leave in the morning. They walked solemnly along the path holding hands. Neither felt the urge to talk. They reached their bench and sat. David put his arm around Grace's shoulders and Grace slid closer to him.

They were sitting quietly enjoying the scenery before them, when Grace unexpectedly asked David, "Did you really have a mental list?"

"What?" David asked surprised as he sat up a little straighter and looked at her. He was holding back the threatening smile as he recalled the incident. "Has that been on your mind since our first meeting?" He paused a moment and asked, "Well, what do you think?"

"I doubted it at the beginning of the meeting, but when I forced you to take over, you did seem to have an agenda….So, did you or did you not have a list? Time to confess," she said jovially.

"Well," David said hesitantly, "I didn't exactly have a list like yours. I had thought about the project and decided the procedure we needed to follow." He then laughingly confessed, "I knew you didn't believe me. But it was a lot of fun pretending."

She gave him a slight punch to his shoulder and said lightly, "You were so exasperating sitting there just nodding your head in approval to my suggestions and not speaking at all."

"Yeah, well—What about you poking your finger into my chest when we first met?"

"You've got to be kidding!" she responded laughing. "That was a defense action! You were walking backwards and were about to trample me.... Anyway, I didn't really hit your chest or make contact with you in any manner. You stopped and turned just in time to face me."

"Now, that's where you're mistaken," David said a bit more seriously. "You see, when that finger was so close to my chest I felt it touch and captivate my heart and that has remained with me to this day and probably will for the rest of my life!"

Those unexpected words brought an emotional tear to her eyes and she could hardly speak. However, she lovingly gazed at him and responded, "Yes, we did get off to a difficult start, but when you walked away and turned around coming back to me with that overwhelming smile of yours and with your hand extended in an effort of apology, as well as indicating 'let's start over' all my annoyance vanished. Then you shook my hand and I cherish to this day that captivating warmth that I felt in that magical moment."

David drew her a little closer with his arm that was around her shoulders. He swallowed hard trying to keep control of his feelings... He gazed into her beautiful face. With his other hand he caressingly ran his fingers through her hair and then he gently touched her chin and with loving eyes he whispered, "I love you Grace! I want you in my life forever!"

She responded by returning his gaze of love and putting her arms around his shoulders as her fingers gently stroked the back of his neck and emotionally whispered, "I love you too! I can't imagine not having you in my life!"

David bent his head down and his lips met hers in the magical kiss of true love!

They remained on the bench enveloped in the joy of a love blessed by God until the sun disappeared from sight. It was time to leave their favorite spot. They would return some other day, hopefully not in the too distant future.

Epilogue

David and Grace followed the road God had provided for them. At this time their road split, taking them in different directions.......But, as roads go, they often come back together and meld into one road again!

Groups of Sing His Praises surfaced and multiplied across the land...even in places that David and Grace had never visited.

As we are well aware, the road is never completely smooth and straight. It has curves, steep hills, pot-holes, rough surfaces and...many times an unexpected surprise awaits on the other side of a sharp blind turn. So it was for David and Grace.

Dear Reader,

It is sometimes difficult to know which road God wishes us to take. But if we follow in true faith the example Jesus set and follow His teachings ...

along with making sure we have quiet, uninterrupted time to listen for God's voice and feel His love, …it will become clear to us.

I wish you God's Blessings and that in faith you will find your "Right Road."

Show me the right path, O Lord; point out the right road for me to follow. Lead me by Your truth and teach me, for You are the God who saves me. All day long I put my hope in You. Psalm 25:4-7

Ruth Jenkins